T0247498

THE EVOLUTION OF SHADOWS

Jason Quinn Malott

UNBRIDLED BOOKS

This is a work of fiction. The names, characters, places and incidents are either the product of the author's imagination or are used fictitiously, and any resemblance to actual persons living or dead, business establishments, events, or locales is entirely coincidental.

Unbridled Books

Library of Congress Cataloging-in-Publication Data

Malott, Jason Quinn.
The evolution of shadows / Jason Quinn Malott.
p. cm.
ISBN 978-1-932961-84-3
1. War photographers—Fiction. 2. Americans—Bosnia and Hercegovina—Fiction 3. Sarajevo (Bosnia and Hercegovina)—Fiction. I. Title.
PS3613.A467E86 2009
813'.6—dc22
2009012546

3 5 7 9 10 8 6 4 2

Book Design by SH • CV

Second Printing

We use each other like axes to cut down the ones we really love.

· Lawrence Durrell, *Justine*

There are betrayals in war that are childlike compared with our human betrayals during peace.

· Michael Ondaatje, *The English Patient*

Contents

Shadows

Lian hears the wind in the trees outside and the creak of the house as its timbers contract in the cool night. The sound fades and comes back like the false sound of the ocean in a seashell. She lies in the small bed the same way she did as a child, her arms crossed over her chest and the arches of her feet pressed together. It's the position of a corpse, and she once thought it would fool the ghosts into believing she was already dead.

She tries not to think of Emil downstairs. He has told her he is sometimes unable to sleep and she shouldn't be concerned by the sound of him pacing the house, but she can't hear anything that sounds human. Only the wind and the creaking house. She tries to think of Gray, the man she has come to find. The way his voice sounded in the morning. The smell of his body, like a warm orange. Even in the dark she can see the small box in the corner of the room that holds Gray's belongings, which Emil has given to her. The journal. The binder full of photos of her. Some clothes she had held to her face the first night, searching for the ghost of his scent. This is how she pulls back from the sounds of the house and drifts to sleep, her hands turning cold against her chest.

Downstairs, Emil prowls, a prisoner of his memories. At night, with the silent accusation of her presence in the house, he feels as if he is constantly breaking the surface of water, exploding air out of his lungs and sliding underneath again. He counts his steps as he paces. It's nine steps across the main room as he moves around the furniture and past the green-painted wall where his uncle was shot. He steps into the kitchen, over the place where his father's blood had collected in the low spot by the entry, and takes another nine steps to the door that opens onto the small, dark garden behind the house. Beyond the garden are five grave markers, the dark silhouettes rising up from the ground. Sometimes he dreams there is a sixth. The one for Mira.

He turns, goes back nine steps across the kitchen to the main room. Nine steps to the front door, which he opens as if expecting the dead. There is only the night air. The smell of dry grass and the faint, old smell of death.

Lian squints against the morning sunlight and looks out the kitchen window and watches Emil in the garden as he uses a piece of twine to tie the limp stem of a tomato plant to a stick he has pushed into the ground. He bends over and pulls weeds from around the plants, then throws them onto a compost heap next to the small garden. At times he will stop, look up past the plum trees and toward the hills to the east. She wonders what he is looking for.

When he reaches the end of the tiny garden he stands, looks at the house, and waves to her. He returns along the row of plants and picks two ripe tomatoes, carries them to the house and up the steps to the kitchen door. She turns to him as he comes in and places the tomatoes on the counter in front of her.

"I am sorry that we must keep waiting," he says. "I had hoped Jack would arrive the same day as you."

"It's fine," she says and looks out the window again at the green markers, the white writing on them. "Emil, why are there graves there?"

"There was no more room in the cemetery."

She looks at her hands where they rest on the counter. They seem connected to some other body.

"It must have been horrible," she says, but he is already moving away and into the main room. She hears the front door open and close softly. After waiting a moment, she leaves the kitchen and climbs the stairs to her room. She closes the door and sits on the bed, takes the photographs from her suitcase. A few months ago these photographs were hidden in binders that were packed in boxes, like secrets in exile, in the basement of her home back in America. She had no need to bring them with her, but they found their way into her suitcase, and she is glad of it. She shuffles them until she finds her favorite. It shows a man, his hair the color of mahogany, asleep on his back with the bed sheets pushed down to his bare hips. One hand rests on his stomach between his navel and the sparse patch of dark hair across his chest. His other hand near his face.

She had stood over Gray on the bed, naked, with his camera in her hands. The loud click of the shutter startled her. He looked up at her then, his eyes wet, and she wanted to dip her tongue in them to see if they tasted like chocolate.

That'll be a good picture, he said.

You're beautiful, she said and eased down to her knees so that she straddled him and pinned him down. *Don't you dare hide this picture from me.*

If you want that picture developed, it's going to cost you.

Yeah? How much?

She felt his hands slip along her thighs to her waist. So little pressure to make her lean down over him. The camera dropped on the pillow beside them. He kissed her while she moved her hands down his stomach and pushed away the sheet.

She hears Emil call her name from the hallway and she presses her hands to her face, rubs the memory from her eyes before finally getting up from the bed to open the door.

"A messenger has come from the village. I will need to go back to Sarajevo to get Jack."

"How long will you be gone?"

"The rest of today, part of tomorrow."

"I'll wait here then, if that's all right."

He nods, then turns and walks down the short hall to the stairs. Lian follows him down, her arms folded across her chest. From the open front door she watches him climb into the old Land Rover and hears the engine start. There is someone in the truck with him she doesn't know. It must be the person who brought the message that Jack had called. Maybe he is the same person who took her call the other day. She realizes she's never been anywhere without a phone before coming here.

Emil backs the truck around and starts down the narrow dirt track to the road that leads to the village. When the truck reaches the road, Lian closes the door to the silent house and stands in the main room staring at the bullet holes in the green wall.

Even though she had not been Ms. Jiang for nearly four years, the letter began:

> *Dear Ms Jiang:*
>
> *I am Emil Todorović. During the war in Bosnia-Herzegovina, I was an interpreter and friend to Gray Banick. I have some of his possessions and know that he wrote to you from time to time. I am trying to locate him, but have not seen him since July 1995. If he is not alive, do you know where I might send his belongings?*
>
> *Emil*

The letter arrived at her office, like the letters Gray had sent. She kept it in her purse for nearly a week until she finally decided to respond. Several attempts ended in the trash before she settled on something simple and direct, something that would not betray the panic caused by the possibility of Gray's death.

> *Dear Mr. Todorović;*
>
> *I have not heard that Gray is back in the area, nor that he*

is dead. I never knew his family. Perhaps he has decided to live elsewhere.

Sincerely, Lian Zhao

The gap in her memory she'd created in order to forget Gray filled, and she couldn't stop thinking about him, about what might have happened to him. As his presence began to nest itself in the shadows at night, it became difficult to lie next to her husband. The lazy way Daniel dropped his arm over her made her feel no better than a pillow. His soft skin and faint hospital smell irritated her. She began to slip out of bed at night and drift down the hallway in the dark to the living room. She would curl up on the couch, a blanket pulled over her shoulders, and fall asleep there only to wake up thinking of Gray. All the ways he could have died.

When Daniel asked, she told him that she was restless and didn't want to wake him.

After the second week of sleeping on the couch, she told him: *I have to go to England.*

I've always wanted to see England, he said.

You don't need to come. It's business.

He set down his coffee mug, looked at her. She watched his eyes move.

It wouldn't be that difficult for me to get time off.

It's for work. I won't have any time to spend with you.

We can take a few extra days, can't we?

She frowned and looked away from him, out past the kitchen doorway to the darkness of the living room.

Daniel, I just want to go to London and do what I have to do and come back.

Why not make it into a vacation for us?

I just want to do business and leave. Can't I do this alone?

You do everything alone, Lian. He got up from the table and walked out of the kitchen.

She thinks of that as she lies awake in Emil's house and waits for the sounds she heard the previous night. There is the wind in the trees outside. The wind racing under the eaves of the house. Nothing else but her breathing.

It is too difficult to sleep, so Lian gets out of bed, goes downstairs in the dark. There are only the sounds of her feet pressing the floor. The wind outside. She feels a tingle, like soft cotton slipping over her skin, as she steps into the kitchen and reaches for the light switch. The feeling stops her. She stares into the darkness trying to discern a shape, not yet afraid. The tingle moves along her arm to her shoulder and tightens the muscles along her back. She turns on the light, expecting to see what had brushed against her in the dark. Nothing.

She crosses the kitchen and takes a glass from the cupboard, fills it with water from the faucet. She leaves the light on in the kitchen as she goes out and climbs the stairs. On her way, she turns on more lights. In her room, she leaves the glass on the old chair by the bed and starts back along her trail of light to the kitchen. She pauses in the main room and looks at the green wall. Then, slowly, she begins to turn out the lights, stepping from empty blackness into the safety of other lights.

If this were her house, she might give in to the superstitions her mother still clung to and which she herself had dismissed long ago.

She would burn oil and lard in bowls and fan the smoke into every corner, chasing off the ghosts and spirits that seem to haunt these rooms.

Again, in the dark, there are no sounds outside her room and the tension will not leave her body. In bed, she presses the arches of her feet together and holds her arms tightly across her chest.

Don't you believe in something, Gray?

I believe in a lot of things, just not religion or ghosts.

So what is it that you do believe in?

Do you want my real answer or my flip answer?

Real, you jerk.

The only intangible thing I try to believe in is love, but it doesn't always work.

What do you mean it doesn't always work?

It's never permanent, he said.

I think it can be.

Emil drives out of the night and into the lighted streets of Sarajevo. Life has come back to the city, but he doesn't think it will ever completely recover. Something was amputated, both out there in the streets and somewhere within himself. As he guides the truck through the city, he passes intersections he once knew for their exposure to the hills. The number of people killed trying to cross. There seem to be no other memories but these.

Emil steers the vehicle into the small parking lot of the Holiday Inn, then down the ramp to the underground garage. There are not many cars inside. He parks near the entrance, shuts off the engine, and sits for a moment looking at the door leading to the stairs.

Twice now in the last week he has been here, and both times the place has seemed empty despite the hundreds of people staying in the rooms above. During the war, there had been a kind of desperate, panicked existence here. The manic coming and going of reporters and photographers. The U.N. officials in their blue helmets and flak jackets who gave their briefings as if there weren't explosions going off outside. Some of them seemed like children playing at war, excited by the mortuary playground Sarajevo had become.

He climbs out of the truck and walks across the hollow cavern to the door. He pushes it open and enters the stairwell. As he climbs to the ground floor, his footsteps echo off the walls. When he comes out of the stairwell, he pauses for a moment in the repaired lobby, then heads across the cavernous space to the lounge. All of it still familiar, but now muted in unfamiliar silence.

Jack sits at a table in the back of the lounge, a drink in one hand and a cigarette in the other. Emil had been certain he would find Jack here. During the war, drinking was a necessity. Like smoking, it was a small act of self-destruction that seemed somehow sane compared to the destruction around them.

To Emil it seems Jack has shrunk since the war. The angles of his face are sharper, as if he has been starving himself, and his hair is thinner. Gray as old snow. There is a cane hooked on the edge of the table, and Emil is glad there will be no wheelchair to deal with.

He sits down and tries to avoid staring at the cane by Jack's elbow. The gunshot memories. He concentrates on the pack of Marlboros.

"Long time since I saw you, Jack."

The old man laughs, holds up the pack of Marlboros. Emil takes one and lights it with the lighter Jack slides across the table.

"I can't believe I got up the nerve to come back." He holds his cigarette and glass in the same hand, drinks, then sets the empty glass near the edge of the table. "Did she really come?"

"Yes. She is at the farm now, waiting."

"Why didn't you wait for me here?"

"She arrived two days ago. It costs her no money to stay with me."

Jack shifts his weight around in his chair, clears his throat. "I guess you'll be taking me to the farm then."

"Is that a problem?"

He clears his throat again and looks around the room. "No, I suppose not."

"The bodies are buried."

Jack nods, looks around again, and finally makes eye contact with Emil. "Gray's probably dead, you know."

"Maybe. Maybe not. He was alive when I left him. I heard there is a reporter from Athens who got married to a Bosnian woman and is living here in Sarajevo now."

"What does that have to do with Gray?"

"I have to look. So do you. He would have looked for us."

"He wouldn't have left us."

The waitress brings another drink and takes away the empty glass. Emil feels pinned to his seat, trapped by the memory of that final look over his shoulder. A body falling among trees.

"Can finally get good whiskey in this hotel," Jack says.

"Jack?"

"I know. I'm sorry. When are we leaving?"

"Tomorrow morning, if we can," Emil says.

"Good. Gives me a chance to sleep off this drunk I'm working on."

"It will almost be like old times."

"In that case I'll be sure to drink a lot more."

"Fine." Emil crushes out the cigarette, takes the pack of Marlboros, and stands. "Tomorrow."

"You didn't get fundamental on me, did you?"

"No. I must see Katja. Good-night, Jack."

Jack raises his glass and drinks.

Emil waits with his hands in the pockets of his jeans as Katja unlocks the bolts. She opens the door and stands squeezed between the door and the frame.

"You should have let me know you were coming," she says.

"I am sorry. I was not thinking."

She steps aside to let him in, then closes the door. The apartment is dark, with the blinds closed tightly over the windows.

"How long are you staying?"

"Just tonight."

"Then do not touch me."

"I am tired, Katja."

"Yes, of course."

He follows her through the small apartment to her bedroom. Slowly he takes off his shirt and jeans in the dark, then gets into bed with her. She turns away, a body of ice next to him.

He wakes in the morning with Katja pressed against him, her head on his shoulder and her arm across his chest. He watches the angle of early sunlight through the gaps in the window blinds. If he looks hard enough, he can see the patches of plaster where holes in the wall were repaired.

He breathes slowly, feels the pressure in his bladder. He wants to ease her away so he can get out of bed and move to the bathroom. But once she is awake, she won't want to touch him again, and the contact of her body is comforting.

You could move back here, she once told him. *It is not so bad anymore.*

You could always come to the farm.

My students are here, my job.

My job is there.

What? Keeping vigil over dead people?

You keep a vigil as well.

He knows they have never forgiven each other their ghosts.

Finally, he moves her away and gets out of bed. When he returns she has her back toward him, and he lies down to stare at the wings of her shoulder blades.

"I thought you were leaving."

"There is no hurry. Jack will not be awake yet."

"Why do you come here if you hardly stay?"

"This city is terrible to me."

"That is not a reason," she says.

She turns toward him and climbs over his body to get out of bed, walks out of the room. He waits for the click as the bathroom door closes, then gets up again, pulls on his clothes, and walks barefoot to the kitchen to make coffee.

Sarajevo is getting better, he knows, but the new peace is not enough for him. There are too many graves. Too many chances he might find Mira's marker here, where it shouldn't be.

Something should change in his life. He should try to collect the broken threads and make something new the way his grandparents did after the Second World War, and his great-grandparents before them. But what if someone comes to shatter it all again?

He sits at the table as Katja goes past and leans against the counter with her back to him. He watches the edge of her shirt rise and fall along the backs of her thighs as she sighs once, then twice. When the coffee is done, she fills two mugs and brings them to the table.

"Have you been to see Stjepan?" she asks.

"No."

She sips her coffee, then says, "He would like it very much if you visited him more often."

Emil looks into the coffee mug. The light in the room strikes the black surface and reflects his dark silhouette.

"I am not making breakfast for you," she says.

"That is fine."

"I want to make breakfast for you."

He looks at her.

"I want to, but I am not making you breakfast," she says.

"That is fine," he says again.

"When you are done looking for them, then come and talk to me, but we cannot do this anymore."

He looks at the small black pool in his cup. The shadow of himself there. "You deserve that much."

"I deserve more, but that is all I want right now."

The house has lost its ominous feeling with the morning. Lian sits at the table holding a cup of coffee, staring out the open back door at the garden and the row of graves. She wonders what Emil's family was like before the war. The dark idea crosses her mind that she wishes her family to go away permanently, for their expectations of her to come only from mute graves instead of obtuse comments during Sunday dinners. There would be no more vague, disapproving looks when she said something they thought sounded too American. No more suspicious looks from her mother, followed by *Aren't you going to have babies?*

She leans on the table and slips her left hand under the collar of her shirt, touches the jagged scar on her right shoulder. Slowly she traces the pattern until the sensation of touch comes only from her fingertips. *This is someone else's scar,* she tells herself. *Someone else's history.*

She gets up from the table and goes down the steps of the porch and across the yard to the garden. The morning is cool with dew on the ground. Sunlight spills over the horizon, fights through the mass of clouds threatening rain. She kneels in the garden and begins to pull up the small weeds Emil missed the day before. She tosses them onto the nearby compost heap.

Later she sits in the kitchen and watches the rain. Mud dries on her hands and knees, and her hair is heavy with water. She feels peaceful for the moment, comforted by ripping weeds from the ground. She could have been twelve again, kneeling in her mother's garden asking if the weeds had names.

The rain falls in small drops, like needles lancing the ground. The leaves on the tomato plants and the trees rattle. Beads of water meander down the windows. There is a smell with the rain, something she can't place. It's not like the rain in Kansas or Missouri. It's not like the spring rain in Taiwan that kept her trapped in her grandmother's house.

Lian closes her eyes and breathes.

Emil stands in the lobby of the Holiday Inn, waiting. It is empty except for the two employees behind the counter. The relative silence of the place is strange to him, as if he has suddenly gone deaf. He glances at his watch, looks toward the stairs, then the elevator. He had not expected Jack to be on time, but it has been half an hour since he came to wait.

He walks to the front desk. "*Zadovoljiti,* would you ring Jack MacKenzie's room?"

The desk clerk nods, hands the phone to Emil, then dials the room number. Emil listens to it ring.

"No answer?" the desk clerk asks.

"One moment."

The receiver is picked up, and Emil hears Jack mumble something that sounds roughly like *Fuck off,* then there is the dial tone. Emil hands the phone back to the clerk.

"He is there. The room number, please?"

"Two-ten."

"Will you come with me and bring a key?"

"Is there trouble?"

"He might be very ill."

Emil and the desk clerk ride the elevator to the second floor, then walk down the quiet hall to Jack's room. The clerk unlocks the door, and they step inside.

After the silent order of the lobby, the mess Jack has made of the room is like an explosion from the war. The mattresses of the two double beds are propped against the windows. Several beer bottles and a scotch bottle lie empty on the floor. There are candles on the table burned down to pale wax pools.

Jack is curled up with his arm over the naked waist of a sleeping woman. His white boxers are bunched up on his pale thighs, and Emil can see the thick pink scars along both of Jack's legs. His arm is dark brown, but the woman is darker, a brunette originally, her hair dyed blond. The sheets are rumpled below her knees, and her small breasts sit high on her chest.

"Is room service working?" Emil asks.

The clerk nods, and Emil can tell he is staring at the woman.

"Have them send up coffee and scrambled eggs with extra toast, please."

"On his bill?"

"Yes, of course."

The clerk leaves and closes the door.

Emil takes hold of one of the mattresses, tugs it away from the window, and lets it flop on the floor. Light bursts into the room and slaps them across their faces. The woman comes awake first, sits up, blinking against the sunlight. She doesn't cover herself.

"Dobro jutro," Emil says.

The woman frowns at him, shakes Jack by the shoulder. He struggles awake and tries to pull the woman against him, but she pushes his hand away and says something to him. Emil thinks the language sounds familiar but can't place it.

"Shit," Jack says. He pushes himself up and covers his eyes with his hand.

Emil lights a cigarette as he leans against the windowsill. The woman says something to Jack again, and he finally responds, struggling to get the words out. She gets out of bed when he finishes and begins to look around for her clothes.

"Looks like you have been enjoying yourself, Jack," Emil says.

"Fucking bastard," Jack says.

"Where is she from?"

"Portugal."

"Interesting."

"She also speaks a little Serbo-Croat."

"A long way from home."

"Aren't we all?"

"I meant for a hooker."

The naked woman steps in front of Emil as she pulls up a pair of heavy denim shorts. She glares at him.

"Hooker?"

"You," Emil says.

"Fuck you, asshole," she says and turns away to slip on a thick sweatshirt.

"That's all she seems to know in English," Jack says. "And she's with the Red Cross."

Emil listens to her speak to Jack as she ties up the laces of her hiking boots. When she leaves, she raises her middle finger to Emil and says something before she pulls the door shut.

"What did she say?"

"She'll look me up when she gets to England," Jack says, then pauses as he rubs his face with both hands. "And you can go fuck a retarded dog, I think, was the rest of it. My Portuguese was never that detailed."

"She seems like a nice girl. Would your wife approve?"

"The divorce means she doesn't have to care. What time is it?"

"A little after nine."

"Are we late?"

"Late? No. A little off schedule."

Jack slides to the edge of the bed, then stands. He sways a little, as if in a breeze.

"I guess I should clean up," he says.

"Go take a shower. I will take care of this."

Jack goes into the bathroom, and Emil hauls a mattress back onto the box springs. He picks up the bottles and stuffs them in the wastebasket. Under the desk chair he finds a condom package carefully stuffed with used rubbers and throws it in the trash. He scrapes the wax puddles off the table, but the spots where the wax had been are now lighter than the rest of the table. He wonders if Jack will try to convince them it was from the war. Back then none of this would have been a problem. People's bad habits and slobbishness were hidden in the general disarray of the siege.

Emil is dragging the second mattress back into place when Jack comes out of the bathroom wrapped in a towel and goes to the backpack where it sits on the floor.

"So, Lian showed up two days ago?"

"Yes. The same day you were supposed to arrive."

"Right. I ran into problems."

"Of course. Problems. Was it the divorce you did not tell me about?"

"I don't want to talk about it."

"Fine."

Emil sits in the chair and crosses his legs. He watches Jack take a few clothes out of his pack and return to the bathroom.

"What's she like?"

"Punctual."

"Yeah, right where we left off," he says. "I can't leave here naked."

Jack follows Emil into the house, and his eyes catch on the bullet holes in the wall of the main room. If he had the desire, or the artistic skill, he could take a pen and draw the outline of the man who had been standing there.

"Lian?" Emil says into the dark house.

Jack closes the door, sets down his backpack. He can't stop staring at the wall. There had been blood there once, and the wall had been white. The bullet marks, which would have been bone-white scars, are now pale green. He takes a deep breath, testing the air for the smell of decay. It's still there, faintly.

For a moment, he feels the same small surge in his chest that he once felt in the presence of gunfire and death. He'd become addicted to it during the wars he'd covered. Then it goes, slips away from him like water over glass. He reaches for the flask in his pocket and is about to draw it out when Emil returns with the woman.

Lian, right? Jack held the photograph to the flickering light.

Gray reached across the table and took the photograph from him. *Yes.*

Why'd you leave her to come here?

Why'd you leave your wife to come here?

This last time? I figure it's safer here.

It was something like that, Gray said and tucked the photograph into his inside jacket pocket.

The woman from the photograph moves across the room toward him now, no longer a creased image studied under dim light. As Emil introduces them, Jack has the feeling she is examining him, a bug pinned to a collector's board, assessing all the faults and breaks in him. He takes his hand away from the flask and wipes it on his pant leg before he offers it to her.

"It's nice to finally meet you," he says. "For a while I wasn't sure you were real."

"I am," she says and looks away from him. When she looks back, the feeling he had is gone.

"Come on, I'll show you to a room," Emil says and picks up the backpack.

Jack follows him up the stairs, aware of Lian watching him struggle up the steps. At the top, he follows Emil down the short hallway and into a room at the very end. He looks to make sure Lian hasn't sneaked up behind them, then sits down on the old bed and rubs his left knee. Emil stands by the door, his arms folded across his chest.

"Jesus, Emil. Why did she come all the way out here?"

"I do not know. I wrote to her because I thought Gray might have gone back to America."

"If he even got out of Potočari."

“We were separated in the woods,” Emil says, and Jacks sees him look down at his feet, then back toward the stairs.

“Emil.”

“I do not think he is dead anymore.”

“Why? Because there’s some reporter from Greece who got married?”

“No. But there were letters from a woman in Paris in the things he left here before we went to Srebrenica. The letters were dated after he came back to Bosnia. When he was waiting for us in Travnik.”

“Suzzette Boisson?”

“Yes. I wrote to her. Who is she?”

“A French reporter Gray had a thing with. Before you started working for him. Did she write back?”

“No. Nothing, but the letters have not been returned either.”

“This is ridiculous. He’s gone, Emil.”

“Then why did you come?”

Jack squeezes his eyes shut, takes a deep breath. “I don’t know. Because you said she was coming, and . . .” He shrugs and looks away.

“And?”

“And I guess I hope we can find him.”

“Get some rest, Jack. You still look like shit.”

“Emil?” Jack pulls the flask out of his jacket. “This isn’t one of the rooms where . . . you know.”

“No. Get some rest,” he says and turns to leave.

Jack stretches out on the bed and closes his eyes.

He wakes up to a dark room and a sense of being lost. It had been dusk when he arrived, and he wonders how late it is now. A dim light slips up the stairs from the main room. It carries the sound of voices like a distant, weakly tuned radio. Slowly he sits up and searches for his jacket in the dark. He finds it, takes out the flask, and opens it. A small sip of whiskey turns into two, then three before he screws the cap back on and puts the flask in the back pocket of his pants. He stands up, finds his cane against the wall, and leans on it for a moment before moving to the door.

Laughter as he descends. The faint sound of a bottle being set on a table. Jack reaches the bottom of the stairs and turns to face the main room, dark and empty. Light comes from the kitchen, almost undulating with the quiet conversation. He limps to the doorway, and the voices fall silent.

An older woman is with them, a glass of *šljivovica* on the table in front of her. It takes a moment for Jack to recognize Hiba. Almost three years since he saw her last, and it seems she has aged a decade.

"Did we wake you?" she asks.

"No." Jack smiles. "It's good to see you again."

"I saw the lights and was feeling lonely." She rises from her chair and hugs Jack.

When she releases him, they both sit down at the table. Emil pours a bit of *šljivovica* into a glass and gives it to Jack. He takes the glass of plum brandy and sips, closes his eyes and lets it sit on his tongue for a moment before he swallows.

"I'm sorry to have interrupted," Jack says.

"I was only telling Lian how you and Emil and Gray rented rooms from me during the war. How quiet he was when you and Emil were not around."

"He was always very quiet," Lian says.

"He did not speak of himself very often with me. Always with his camera taking pictures. One morning, I remember, I found him behind the house sitting on an old chair watching the sunrise. It was a cold morning, and he was only wearing jeans and an undershirt. I believe he was taking pictures of the sunrise and the hills where the Serbs sat with their guns pointed at our town. He had been up most of the night, listening to them, he said."

"That was near Travnik," Emil says.

"Yes. I used to live there with my husband."

"Did your husband fight?" Lian asks.

"Yes, he was killed by the Chetniks."

"I'm sorry," Lian says.

"Please, do not apologize. We always ask about the dead."

Jack stares into his cup and tries to remember the morning Hiba has described. He doesn't doubt her memory, but his own. It could have been one of the nights he drank himself to sleep. Or it could have been one of the nights he spent trying to reach his wife by satellite phone only to have her hang up on him. If he had a photograph of some part of that night, he could fit the pieces together into a half-imagined memory, except he has nothing. He drinks his glass empty and pours a little more.

"I should be going. It is late," Hiba says. "I hope you are feeling well soon, Jack."

"I feel fine," Jack says. "I guess I was more tired than I thought. I'm sorry I slept through most of your visit."

"Perhaps next time," she says. "You will come back, I hope?"

"Yes," he says, even though it feels like a lie.

She gets up from the table and, as she walks past him, places a hand on Jack's shoulder. "Things are always different than when you left them," she says.

Jack reaches up to touch her hand where it rests on his shoulder, but she is already moving away. He listens to her and Emil go through the main room to the front door and say good-bye.

"Where do we begin?" Lian asks when Emil comes back to the kitchen.

"The last I saw Gray was in the woods near Potočari, north of Srebrenica," Emil says. "But that area is the Republic of Srpska now, and it is still dangerous for Muslims."

"But the war's over," Lian says.

"The wars are never really over here," Jack says. "And the Bosnian Serbs have never liked to have journalists around. We tend to fuck up their plans for genocide."

"Will it be dangerous?" she asks.

"Perhaps," Emil says.

Jack gets up from the table and goes to the black window to look out at the night. The pain in his legs is distant, numbed by the alcohol. He tries to catch a glimpse of Hiba moving down the road to her house, but clouds hide the moon and everything along the ground has disappeared into black.

"What time are we leaving tomorrow?" Jack asks.

"Early," Emil says.

"Then I should go back upstairs and get some sleep."

Jack turns from the window and takes the flask out of his back pocket. He opens it and takes a drink before he starts out of the kitchen on his way back to his room.

Lian pushes her sunglasses closer to her eyes, then wraps her arms around her knees. She rests her chin on her right knee and stares at the pile of clouds over the village they passed through a little while ago. Jack sleeps on the grass next to her, his right arm over his face to keep out the sun. Emil is leaning into the engine compartment of the Land Rover.

"Are you sure there isn't something I can do?"

"No, it is a simple thing."

She nods, looks down at Jack.

"Is he going to drink like that the whole time?"

Emil takes his arms, streaked with dirt and grease, out of the engine compartment and wipes them with an old rag. He walks over and sits on the ground next to Jack.

"He might. I think things have been difficult for him since the war."

"Did he always drink like this?"

"During the war everyone drank when they could. There was nothing else to do."

She nods. "Is it fixed?"

"For the moment," Emil says. "It will be hard to find a new hose."

"Will it get us to Potočari?" She smiles at him.

"I do not know if it will get us fifty meters."

"That's not very reassuring," she says.

Emil drops the dirty rag on Jack's chest, but he doesn't move.

The wind slips along the valley, draws the clouds from the village over them. There is the smell of approaching rain. Lian looks at the clouds, foam white across the top and dark underneath. The trailing patch of shade slides against the ground like a wraith.

"How did you meet Gray?" she asks.

Emil laughs. "You ask a lot of questions. Were you ever a reporter?"

"No. I'm sorry."

"I do not mind. I met Gray while urinating against a building."

Nearly a hundred people had crammed into the basement of an old office building. The space lit mostly by candles. A teenaged boy with one leg played cassette tapes on a portable stereo. The pockets of his jacket bulged with extra batteries. There was beer and *šljivovica*. The collection of bodies pushed around each other, and a space was left in the center of the basement for those who wanted to dance.

Emil had arrived late, his travel slowed by a sniper attack along one of the streets he had to cross. He wedged himself inside, grateful for the warmth of so many bodies together, and refused the bottle of *šlivo* someone offered him. Instead he traded some of his cigarettes for a beer and stood with it against his chest in the dim light. The staccato snap of rifle fire in the distance confused the rhythm of the music.

Earlier that night, as he'd sat quietly in his apartment staring at the boards he'd nailed over the windows, he had heard someone in the hallway mention the party. He knew he could not sit in that apartment and continue to think about Mira, about what might have happened to her, and not drive himself insane. He wanted the noise of a party, the sounds of people trying to be normal. Anything but the semisilence of his living room, where his cousin spent most of his days staring at nothing.

Refugees from the small villages in the path of the Bosnian Serbs had been coming into Sarajevo since the start of the war, and nearly all of the women told of rape. They told how their friends or sisters were taken as trophies while the others were sent on. They told stories of massacres and executions. Somehow Emil had felt separate from them, untouchable, until Stjepan had arrived.

News about the massacre of his village had found its way to Sarajevo weeks before, carried by the few survivors who knew the way better than a boy could. Emil had expected tragedy. But what Stjepan told Emil was worse than tragedy and left him numb and restless for days. Their family had been killed and Emil's fiancée, Mira, taken away. Emil was certain she was dead, but he could do nothing to stop the agony of hope.

He had believed something like this couldn't happen to his family. Their history, already shot through with too much death, seemed to demand God keep such horrors from revisiting them. There had been ten children in the Todorović family before World War II. The oldest had died in a Nazi concentration camp because he'd been a prominent Communist Party member in Zagreb. Two died fighting for Tito's Partisans. Five more, boys and girls, had been slaughtered by the Nazi-backed Ustashe in a raid because their surname was Serbian. Only Emil's father and uncle survived the war. Their mother had carried the infants off to hide in the hills. Her lesson learned when members of her family had been murdered after the First World War simply for being Muslim.

It had been foolish to think there could be an exception for his family. It seemed their heritage doomed them to suffering because they were Serbs who had come to Bosnia and become Muslims. He would go and get drunk and wipe it all out of his mind, if he could.

There seemed to be plenty of beer that night, and as he drank one after another, he began to shrink and expand at the same time. The room was no longer so crowded, and he felt that his body seemed to take up less space, yet he felt like he was engulfing everything, seeing it all as it happened around him. His mind, like a radio halfway tuned to a station, slipped along the edges of sound.

The sudden bolt of a camera flash made him blink. He rubbed his eyes and drew himself back together before turning to climb the stairs out of the basement. As politely as he could, he pushed past the people crowded on the steps smoking cigarettes. Behind the smokers a few couples clutched together to make whatever privacy they could in the gray, half-lit stairwell. Near the top, Emil decided he would begin his trip home. Nothing kept him from thinking of her, and if he drank any more he'd only get shot wandering home in the cold.

Outside, he checked the location of the hills to make sure he could not see them, then stepped up to the wall of a demolished building and unzipped his pants. Another person came to stand next to him.

His bladder empty, Emil zipped up and started to turn away.

Do you speak English? the man asked.

Yes, Emil said, and turned to look at him. A camera hung from the man's neck, a camera bag slung across his shoulders. A dark ball cap was pushed back on his head.

How would you like a job?

Doing what?

The man finished urinating and zipped up his pants, looked back to the doorway of the basement, then at Emil. *I need a new interpreter. The man who worked for me was killed by a sniper.*

Why me? Do I look bulletproof?

No, the man said.

How do I know you will not get me killed?

You don't. Look, it's a hundred dollars a week. That's all I can afford. If you want the job, be at the Holiday Inn tomorrow morning.

American?

Yes.

I will think about it.

Good. What's your name?

Emil Todorović.

Gray Banick.

Emil shook Gray's hand and then began his long, slow walk home.

Lian sits in the passenger seat of the Land Rover and watches the road slowly being eaten by the front of the truck. She tries not to worry about the sounds coming from the engine. The slowly rising temperature gauge she is sure Emil is watching too.

"How did you meet Gray?" Emil asks.

She smiles. "I was in an antique bed race."

Lian sat in the middle of the platform dressed in white shorts and a white tank top, a yellowed wedding veil over her face, as they waited at the starting line with three other teams. The four guys from engineering stood at the corners, silent. In the course of the afternoon, it seemed they had all run out of things to talk about with her. She looked out at the crowd lining the street, which had been blocked off for this event of the festival. She covered her mouth and yawned, her eyes squeezed shut with the effort. She was ready to go home.

When the yawn passed, she opened her eyes and there was a photographer standing in the crowd looking at her, laughing. She tried to watch him without staring. He was tall and seemed to be nothing but sharp angles and planes. The color of his hair reminded her of stained wood, or cinnamon. She watched him step through the crowd and move down the street to the finish line. He removed the lens from the camera as he walked, placed it in his camera bag, then snapped on a long telephoto lens. He walked deliberately, without hesitating or shuffling around people. *He moves like a wolf,* she thought. He stopped in the center of the road, just beyond the finish line, and waited.

Finally the beds were pushed to the starting line. The starter took his place on the sidewalk, raised the cap pistol, and fired. The four beds lurched forward, and Lian sprawled back against the frame. Her eyes were fixed on the photographer down the road, his camera raised to his eye and pointed in her direction. She stuck out her tongue and crossed her eyes.

He moved to his left and up onto the sidewalk as the beds rushed across the finish line. Lian's team came in second. As the runners stood by the bed, hands on their hips and breathing hard, Lian got off the platform and pulled the veil off her head. The photographer was coming over to them, a notepad and a pen in his hands.

I'm Gray Banick, with the Star, he said and put the pen in his mouth to shake her hand, then took it out before he spoke again. *I'd like to get your name for the captions on these pictures just in case we end up using them.*

Did you get me yawning?

He smiled. *I did.*

Great, she said. *I'm sure that'll be the one you use.*

I could use the one of that face you made.

She tossed the veil onto the bed. *That'd be cute.*

Would you rather I not publish your name?

She shrugged. *Lian Jiang,* she said and spelled it for him. He stopped the other people on Lian's team and took down their names too. Then he reached into a pocket of his camera bag, brought out a business card, and handed it to her. *Is there a number where I can reach you in case I need to double-check anything?*

Double-check?

Just in case. Make sure I've got the right names with the right faces.

She smiled at him, gave him her pager number. He wrote it on his notepad, then stuffed it in his camera bag, but he kept standing there as if he had more to say.

Are you going to be shooting pictures here the rest of the day?

Unless there's a fire, or shootout, or something else tragic.

How fun.

Why do you ask?

The company I work for is sponsoring the concert tonight.

Ah, a little free press?

Yes, sort of.

I'll see you there then, he said.

Good, she said and waved to him as he walked off into the crowd, slipping between the other people as if they were trees.

"Did a picture of you appear in the newspaper?"

"Yes, the yawning picture. My parents saw it and were upset. My mother kept saying she didn't raise her daughter to run around in public half naked."

Emil smiles, then turns his attention to a new sound coming from the engine. Lian glances at the temperature gauge and sees it is pushed over into the red. There is a knocking, then a whining that gets louder until Emil pulls over to the side of the road.

"What now?" she asks.

"I do not know." He shuts off the engine.

In the backseat, Jack sits up and rubs his face with both hands. "Someone shooting at us?"

"Go back to sleep," Emil says and climbs out of the truck.

"Bloody hell," Jack says. "What now?"

"Something's wrong with the engine," Lian says.

"I'm surprised this thing hasn't fallen apart already."

Emil pushes up the hood and is blocked from Lian's view. She sits and listens to him turn and tap things on the engine. He swears in his own language, then there is a sound like stones being dropped on the asphalt. She wonders what problem he has found and is about to open her door and step out when he reappears. He comes to stand at the passenger window and frowns. His hands are dirty with grease again.

"We are now walking," he says.

"Is it that bad?" Lian asks.

"It is," Emil says. "There is a leak."

"Well," Jack says, "maybe someone will come along and we can get a ride."

"Maybe," Emil says. "It would be best if we had our own vehicle. I know someone in Sarajevo who might be able to get us a car."

"Are we closer to Sarajevo or Potočari?" Lian asks.

"Sarajevo."

"Crippled drunk walking. Great," Jack says.

Lian shakes her head and tries to read the expression on Emil's face. It is impossible to tell if he is as angry as he seems. The wink he gives her is nearly conspiratorial, and she wonders if Emil is kidding about the engine only to irritate Jack. When she steps out of the truck her feet touch down on wet pavement, tinted yellow-brown with antifreeze and oil. They take their bags and begin to walk.

They climb down from the back of the old pickup truck and stand on a road overlooking Sarajevo as the truck drives away. Their clothes smell of filthy straw and oily engine exhaust. Above them the sky slowly turns black with the coming night, and a veil of clouds slips over the face of the moon. Lian watches the lights of the city come on, tentative against the darkness.

"I wonder if we'll be able to get a room at the Holiday Inn," Jack says.

"There are other hotels now," Emil says.

Lian sets her suitcase on the grass by the road, sits down on top of it, and looks out over the city. "It's very pretty from up here."

"Right over there is Sniper Alley," Jack says.

She follows his gesture with her eyes to where a wide roadway cuts into the city. She tries to imagine an unseen enemy tracking her with his rifle, finger snug against the trigger.

"It must have been hard to live like that," she says.

"We did not notice after a while," Emil says. "It sometimes seemed only like a game."

"With incredibly high stakes," Jack says.

Emil spits on the ground, picks up his backpack, and slips his arms through the straps. "Sometimes I wish for another war."

"For revenge?" she asks.

Emil shrugs and turns away from her, starts down the road. She and Jack pick up their belongings and follow him down the hill and into Sarajevo.

They find two rooms in a partially restored hotel near the old part of town. Jack and Emil share a double room on the second floor, and Lian takes a smaller room down the hall. The two floors above them are sealed off for repairs.

Lian collapses on the hard bed in her room and stares out the window at the night sky. Exhaustion pulls at her bones, but her eyes won't close; her mind won't slow down and collapse into nothing. There are the stars and the moon out from behind the veil of clouds, crowding into the window frame.

Gray was already at the park when she came back for the concert that evening long ago. The small, nervous voice that whispered in the back of her mind told her she shouldn't look at him, but he was impossible to ignore. She sat down in one of the folding chairs in front of the stage, crossed her legs, and waited for him to notice her from where he stood by the television van. He was talking to one of the local anchormen. Lian knew his face from TV but couldn't remember his name. Finally Gray shook the man's hand and walked away. He didn't even look in her direction.

She put her hand to her forehead. *I'm an idiot,* she said softly, then dropped her hand into her lap and looked up at the sky. There was a small moon, and the stars were faint against the light coming up from the city. A yawn forced its way up, and she covered her mouth with her hand. There was laughter through the noise of people around her, and she turned to see him holding his camera against his chest.

Do you find everything so boring? he asked.

She smiled at him, felt the blood surge to her cheeks. *I don't get much sleep.*

He sat down next to her and slipped his camera into the bag, then pushed it under his chair.

Aren't you going to take any pictures of the concert?

He shook his head, smiled at her for a moment, then turned to the orchestra as it began to warm up.

Her memories finally let her fall asleep, and her dreams are jumbled with images of Gray: his body on the white sheets of her bed. The closeness of his face as his hands push through the hair at her temples and drift back to pull her face to his in the dark. The soft feel of his lips against her stomach. His breath on her neck as he sleeps, spooned against her.

She wakes up in the morning, clutching her pillow, a feeling like a fist in her chest. She wants to go home, to forget about this search. What did she think would happen? A miracle? A romance-story reunion? Had she thought coming to this country would rebuild the things she destroyed? The motivation she had in Kansas City has fallen away from her somewhere over the ocean, and now there is simply inertia, awaiting decay.

They have breakfast in a nearly empty café a few blocks from the hotel. Shirred eggs in tiny cups, coffee, a few slices of warm bread. The overhead lights are bright enough to push back the overcast morning outside, and the odors of cooking, as the café prepares for the afternoon, are strong enough to defeat the prophetic smell of rain. There is little talk among them, and Lian is sure that somehow they know she woke up crying.

She watches Jack pour whiskey into his coffee, then return the flask to his pocket while Emil lights a cigarette and sits looking up at the ceiling. Lian wonders if they know what they are going to do. How can they expect to find any trace of Gray after two years? Things are never found unless they want to be found.

She looks away from the two men, across the café to the entrance and out to the street where a car sits. Exhaust plumes out of the tailpipe. The rain begins. Fat drops shatter on the ground and on the body of the car.

"How long do you think we'll be here?" she asks.

Emil shrugs. "I do not know how long it will take my friend to find a car."

Lian looks at him, and the question spills out of her mouth. "Will it be stolen?"

"You might say the car will be permanently borrowed from the deceased," Jack says. "It's hairsplitting, if it makes you feel better."

"No, not really. Won't anyone care?"

"No," Emil says and crushes out his cigarette.

"Can't we just rent one?" Lian asks.

"Yes, but I will still need something to drive after you are gone."

"And the old Land Rover likely won't be there when he goes back," Jack says.

"Someone will just take it?" she asks.

"Or they will strip it for parts," Emil says. "Or smash it for fun."

"I see."

"I should be going," Emil says.

They get up from the table and step out of the café into the morning rain. Jack is talking to her about the construction around them, but she ignores him. She watches Emil where he stands now, as if he doesn't know them anymore, his head turned up to the sky so the rain splashes against his face. Finally he tilts his head down and looks at Lian, smiles.

"There are a few people I need to see," he says.

"When will you be back to the hotel?" Jack asks.

"Tomorrow," Emil says and looks down the street, away from Lian. "With a car, I hope."

She says nothing, keeps the folded newspaper over her head against the rain.

"Be careful," Jack says.

Emil turns away from them and moves down the street.

Internal Cities

There is the thick smell of cigarettes when the door is opened for him. Emil enters and waits as Goran locks the door before leading him down the hall to the living room.

A man and a woman are asleep on the couch. A confusion of pale skin and dark clothes. Empty plastic bags are scattered across a low board supported by old bricks. A broken piece of mirror sits precariously on the edge of the makeshift table. Goran drops into an old chair, the foam stuffing boiling out of the arms. He finds a pack of cigarettes among the mess and shakes one out, puts it between his lips.

"Need one?" he whispers.

Emil holds up his hand, shows Goran the pack of Marlboros he has, then takes one out and lights it.

"What brings you to see me after so long?"

"I need a car."

Goran smokes his cigarette and stares at Emil. "Why? Are you leaving Bosnia?"

"I am going to Potočari."

"Really? What for?"

"I left something there."

Goran crushes out his cigarette. "Give me one of those Marlboros."

"I have some money if that would make this easier," Emil says and shakes out a cigarette for him.

The woman on the couch moves, rubs her cheek against the man's chest. She squints toward Emil. He knows nothing registers with her and he is only a mumbling form in the dark. When she wakes up he will be a gray memory from her dreams.

"I am offended, Emil. I would give you a car for nothing. I would never make you pay me for anything," Goran says, lighting the cigarette as he speaks. "I will see what I can find. Can you come back this evening?"

Emil nods and waits for Goran to lead him down the hall and unlock the door to let him out.

"Shouldn't he have been reported missing at some point?" Lian asks.

"I'm sure he was, but there are millions missing from this war."

She shrugs. "It just seems strange that he hasn't turned up."

"Lian," Jack limps over to the chair by the window, "there are graves they'll never find."

"So how are we going to find one man?"

Jack sits down and looks out the window at the city, turns the handle of his cane with his fingertips. "Emil hopes he can find the place where they got separated in the woods; maybe there'll be remains, or some sign that he got away. I don't expect we'll find much, and I'm trying not to hope too much that he is alive. I don't want to feel like I've lost him twice."

Lian looks down at her shoes, pulls her hair over her shoulder and twists it into a rope. In the silence of the room she listens to the syncopated rhythm of their breathing. The whisper of her hair through her hands. She sympathizes with Jack but can't find an expression or a gesture to convey her sympathy that doesn't feel like an unveiling of herself.

In her desperation to get here, she hadn't considered what she expected to happen. Now, with motion and Jack's pessimism, everything feels ridiculous, fantastical. A little girl's romantic dream. She tries to decide if she should call Daniel with the truth, tell him where she is and that she is coming home. She uncoils the rope of her hair and separates it through her fingers.

"But I could be wrong," Jack says and pushes himself to his feet. "I think I might lie down for a while, then go find a bar."

She watches him walk across the room to the door, open it, and step into the hall. When the door is closed and she is alone again, she stares at her suitcase. Suddenly none of this feels right to her. It feels crazy. Impulsive. She gets up and leaves her room.

She finds a phone in the lobby and huddles in the corner of the little booth with the receiver pressed to her ear. Across the lobby and through the front window of the hotel, the city, with its repairs and new construction, seems as distant as the moon. She navigates the operators, gives them her home number, and waits. She doesn't expect Daniel to be there until he answers.

"Where are you calling from?" he asks.

"Sarajevo," she says.

A pause as the words they speak travel through space, bouncing off a satellite, through cables halfway around the world. There is enough time that the familiarity of his voice doesn't help her calm down, and the miles obscure his tone that always made her brave enough to desire his absence.

"Bosnia, Lian?"

"Yes."

There is time to think about what he will say.

"What the hell are you doing there?"

She looks past the front desk to the doors that open onto the street. People walk by, and beyond them the cars zip past in flashes.

"Lian," he says, "what are you doing in Sarajevo?"

"I'm . . ." She stops, takes a deep breath as she thinks of something to say.

"You're what?"

"I took a detour."

"A detour? I don't understand."

"I'm sorry I called, Daniel. I'll be home like planned."

"Lian," his voice reaches her, and she stops, waits, "what is going on with you?"

She presses her shoulder hard against the wall of the booth. "I'm sorry."

"Come home, Lian. Whatever you're doing out there, it can't be that important . . ."

She closes her eyes, suddenly hating the sound of his voice. "It is important," she says.

". . . to run around in Bosnia doing whatever it is you're doing." The last of his words reaching her, then, "What's so important?"

"You couldn't understand," she says, and waits for the words to travel around the world to his ears. She knows he will be angry. When he relays the information to her parents, she knows they will panic and think she is having a nervous breakdown.

"I thought things were getting better."

"I'm sorry, Daniel. I'll call again when I can," she says and hangs up the phone.

She rushes back to her room where she falls onto the bed as if she has been struck from behind. Lying there, her eyes closed, she wishes she could take everything back. All the doubt, all the fear. This is what she wants. She's wanted it for years but was always too afraid. That was how she'd ended up like this.

That phone call was a mistake, she knows. She is certain he will come after her because this is the biggest thing she has kept from him.

Daniel holds the buzzing phone in his hand and stares at his feet pressed against the pale-blue carpet. Finally he turns off the phone and drops it on the cushion at his side.

There were a couple of days, after she left, when he wondered if her trip was what she had said it was. He hated to give much weight to those thoughts. Intuition was something listened to only when all logical avenues had failed. That was how he expected life to work. Until her phone call there had been no legitimate reason to think anything had happened other than Lian had gone to London and would return in two weeks.

He shakes his head as he pushes himself up from the couch, then walks down the hallway to their bedroom. The bed, disheveled only on his side, still holds the smell of her perfume in the pillowcases. Her voice still in his ear as he opens the closet. *You couldn't understand.* How could she say that when he has done everything she has asked of him?

He looks at her clothes, her shoes jumbled together on the floor of the closet. *There are always signs of illness,* he thinks. He pulls a pair of shoe boxes off the shelf in the closet and places them on the bed, takes off the lids. They contain nothing but the minutiae of a past life. Figurines and old toys. A delicate seashell the size of a little girl's palm. He holds it to his ear, but there is no sound. There is a clear glass dragon attached to a jagged piece of stone. Silly teenaged stuff. He returns the lids to the boxes and slides them back onto the shelf.

Over the years he has snooped through her things when he could, when her refusal to tell him little secrets has made him frantic. He was afraid of being caught then. Aware that, if she knew he was prying, he might lose her trust. It has not been the type of marriage he wanted to have, but so many things people have aren't exactly what they want. That doesn't make the thing less valuable, just different. He has always wanted to keep jealousy and paranoia away from their relationship, but this is too big to allow space for.

He pulls open the drawers of her bureau and pushes her clothes from side to side, runs his hands along the bottoms. There are tied bundles of potpourri jammed in the corners. The whisper of her scent. Why did she go to Bosnia? Why did she lie to him? *I'll be in London,* she had said.

His hands plunge into the bottom drawer, push aside a few thin sweaters. The feel of paper stops him. He takes the envelope out of the drawer and is sure he's seen it before. The memory hovers at the edge of his mind until he takes the card out of the envelope, and then it snaps into place.

He'd gone out to get the mail that day.

There were a few bills and a small white envelope addressed to Lian. It looked to be a card from the size of it, but there was no return address. Turning it over between his fingers, he closed the front door against the cool air outside and walked to the kitchen where he dropped the bills on the table. He opened the white envelope. It was a plain white card with the word "Congratulations" embossed on the front. The lower right-hand corner was missing, and nothing was written inside. He looked closely at the missing corner. Someone had chewed it off.

Lian? He started down the hallway to their bedroom and stopped when he heard the washing machine rattle in the laundry room. He opened the door. *Lian?*

She stood against the washing machine, a blue t-shirt strangled in her hands. Her eyes seemed to focus somewhere over his left shoulder so that he almost turned to see what she was looking at.

What is this? He held the card out to her, and her eyes snapped onto it, skipped right over him as if he were mist.

I have no idea, she said.

There's nothing in it. No return address. Does this, he waved the missing corner toward her, *mean something?*

No. Throw it away.

Her eyes never left the card, the blue shirt twisted tighter in her hands. He turned away and dropped the card into the wastebasket by the door.

Why had she saved it from the trash? He stands up now and places the card on top of her dresser, turns to look at the room. There is no other place to secret something away. He leaves the bedroom and goes down the hall to the kitchen, where the basement stairs begin.

Four boxes are stacked in a corner of the basement, unopened since she joined him here. There has to be something to explain the sudden weight she assumed around him when at first she had seemed as light as silk laid over skin. It had been like a kind of death just before their marriage, and he is sure it is documented somewhere in her old cardboard boxes. He should have looked through these things a long time ago instead of putting up with her periodic morbid silences, hoping she would snap out of it.

One by one he pulls open the boxes and examines the contents. Lion-headed bookends, a framed photograph of the Golden Gate Bridge. The accumulated debris of a single life. The box with the scrapbooks and photo albums has been opened and resealed. He can tell by the tape. Clear packing tape on all the rest, brown on this one covering the clear.

He sits down on the floor with the photo albums balanced on his lap and opens the first one. The photographs are all from before their wedding. He's seen most of them before, back when they were dating. Pictures of her family and friends. A trip to Taiwan. He turns quickly through the others, finding more pictures that don't mean anything to him. A photo of her yawning that was cut from a newspaper. A few more scattered photographs of her.

With the last album, he begins to study the photos as Lian becomes more of a subject of the camera instead of the shadow behind it. He turns the pages slowly and stares at each photograph. In one, Lian is walking down a street in a red dress Daniel has never seen her wear. In another, she is curled on the floor of her old apartment reading the newspaper and holding a cup of coffee to her lips. In another, Lian is smiling.

She never smiles like that now, he thinks. *Always only half that smile. A wisp.*

Then there is a photograph that seems familiar, as if re-creating something from old Hollywood. In the photo, Lian is sitting in a director's chair, legs crossed, her face passive. Behind her, a mirror where the photographer who took the picture is reflected. The photographer is a white man, his image blurred in the shadows there. The focus is on Lian's pale face, the slow stare back at the camera, or perhaps at the photographer in front of her.

Carefully he removes the photograph and places it on the floor next to him. He recognizes some of the places where she was photographed. They are places she has told him she doesn't want to go. The small Italian restaurant on Lincoln Street. The park where a tiny stream runs, disappearing under footbridges to meet up somewhere with the river running out of town. Every now and then some flickering image of the man taking the picture. A shadow or a fuzzy back-image that is always like a wraith, a ghost twinned to the aliveness of Lian in these pictures. He runs his fingers over the places where photographs are missing and wonders what they might have been.

Finally there is one he is certain is of the photographer, or part of him. The photographer had to have been almost on top of the subject.

One hand lifted to cover his right eye. A half smile. Daniel takes the photograph out of the album.

"Do you know who this man might be?" Daniel asks Lian's sister.

Kay takes the photographs from him, shuffles them in her hands. "No, why?"

"I found them at home. Are you sure you don't know who he is?"

Kay shakes her head, hands the photographs back to him. "I wish I knew something more to tell you."

Daniel takes his glasses off and pinches the bridge of his nose. "Why would she tell me she was going to London and then go to Bosnia?"

"I don't know, Daniel. She'll come back."

"But why did she go?"

Kay shrugs, gets up from the couch, and walks to the kitchen. "Would you like some tea?"

"Did you know she has a scar on her right shoulder? Someone bit her."

Kay appears from the kitchen, frowning, a teapot in her hands. "What?"

"Every time I brought it up she refused to talk about it. It drives me mad."

"No, I didn't know."

"You're not going to help me at all, are you?"

She comes back to the couch and sits down. "I'd help you if I could, Daniel, but I don't know why she went to Bosnia. She's good at keeping secrets."

"I have to go," he says.

"You won't stay for tea?"

"I'm sorry, no."

Something changed almost as soon as he proposed, and the quiet *Yes* drifted up from her down-turned face like a surrender. He remembers the moment clearly. The sudden urge to ask her, *Are you sure?* But he ignored it.

Let's wait a few days to tell everyone, she said.

Why?

Please, just a few days.

He gave in and did not see her again for three days. He tried to call her a number of times before he went to her apartment. When she finally opened the door for him, she looked even worse than the night he had proposed.

Have you been sick? he asked, his hands and eyes moved to find some symptom.

No, she said. *I just haven't been sleeping much. It's nothing.*

He put his hands on her shoulders, and she jerked away from him, her eyes closed in pain.

What's wrong?

A crick in my neck.

Let me rub it out.

No, I'll be fine. I just need to finish getting ready.

Five months after he proposed, they were married. He had fallen in love with her because it had felt like she was his silent companion during the Sunday dinners Lian's father had invited him to. Because she had been so easy to be with on the nights they had gone out. But the person he met at the end of the aisle and drove away from the reception with had barely said anything to him for weeks.

After checking into their room at the airport Hilton, where they would spend their wedding night before flying to Jamaica for their honeymoon, he kissed her. He felt her hands against his neck, sweeping across his shoulders, but her body against his was stiff, unyielding. Nothing like before. Clumsiness pursued his hands along the buttons of her dress, and then, as he pulled the dress from her shoulders, he saw the scar. The shape, laid open and obvious to him. Someone had bitten her, put teeth through her skin as if she were meat. As if she weren't even human. He stopped and held her arms in his hands and stared at the scar.

Who did this to you? he asked.

She pulled away from him and sat on the bed, her back angled toward him. The scar glared at him like the ghost of a lost third eye.

I'm not going to tell you.

What?

Daniel, forget about it. It's not what you think.

The statement pounded into him like a wall in the dark a sleeper misnavigates while moving to other parts of the house. He stood there, unable to step toward her, unable to step away. In the hospital he could make a decision quicker than anyone, rescue a person from death on the operating table. He could take the riskiest decision and succeed, but . . .

You're in denial, he said.

I wasn't raped.

But that's brutal no matter what might have happened.

Daniel, if I had been raped, I would have gone to the police.

How did it happen? Who did that?

You don't want the answer to that question, Daniel. Don't ask me that ever again.

She stood up from the bed and dropped her dress to the floor, then walked to the bathroom. When she came back, she was naked, her underclothes held in a bunch in her hand. She dropped them on top of her dress. She was an eclipse, blocking the light from the bathroom behind her. His sight drifted across the tops of her small feet, along her legs to the dark hair below her belly. Her breasts. Her slender neck. Her lips. Her eyes, dark and lost in the white light around her.

It's in the past and doesn't concern you. I've married you, and that's all that matters.

She kissed him then, and when he didn't respond she continued to kiss him until he surrendered, put his arms around her and kissed back. She had chosen him, and he would concede.

Daniel sits in the living room of his house, the photographs he has taken from the albums laid next to him on the couch. His eyes focus and unfocus on the hazy image of the man behind Lian. He should have pressed her more about the scar, demanded the truth from her instead of giving in.

The questions and the lack of answers hang inside him, pulling the edges of his mind into sharp points he stumbles over. He wants an answer, one he can take and use to fill the sudden screaming hollowness in his chest. All of his concern, his patience, his gentleness with her seems to have been wasted.

He watches the light shifting along the wall and up the ceiling as the sun is fractured through the tree in the front yard and again through the curtains. He won't sit and wait for her.

She finds Jack in the bar a few blocks down the street from the hotel, exactly where the note he'd slipped under her door had said he'd be. He is slumped over the table like a turtle, a half-empty glass close to his twitching fingers.

"Jack," she says.

His eyes won't focus on her. "Have you finally come to join me?"

"I'm sorry," she says. "I was trying to sleep."

"It's not too late. Have a seat."

"Jack, let's go."

"Go where?"

"Back to the hotel."

"But dear, I've been unable to make it to the restroom."

Lian frowns, steps closer to his table. She places her hand on his shoulder and eases him back. There is a wet stain spread out from the crotch of his tan slacks.

"What happened, Jack?"

"My legs hurt just a little too much to move," he says. "It's not the first time."

There are not many people in the place. Two men are playing pool in the back, and the bartender is half awake on his stool behind the counter. A woman smokes a cigarette as she stands leaning against the bar; her eyes flick from Jack to Lian, then away as Lian looks at her.

"What do I have to do to get you sobered up, Jack?"

"Well, don't give me any damn coffee. I'll just piss myself again."

She slides out a chair and sits down. Jack takes a pack of cigarettes from his shirt pocket and spills them all onto the table. He stuffs one in his mouth, then pats himself down with limp hands. The heavy Zippo tumbles out of his grasp and onto the table, smashing a few of the cigarettes. "Well, shit," Jack says. "Would you be so kind?"

She picks up the lighter, flips it open, and spins the wheel for the flame. With the cigarette lit, he leans back in the chair and blows smoke at the fans above him.

"God, I feel like such a bloody infant," he says.

Lian isn't sure what to say, so she picks up one of his cigarettes and lights it. The smoke on her throat is harsh and hot. She keeps back her cough as she blows the smoke away.

"You don't smoke, do you?"

"I do now."

"Gray didn't smoke when I met him, but the war gave him the habit. Just like everyone else."

"How does the war make someone smoke?"

"It's either that or go stir-crazy," he says. "And when someone can kill you at any moment, it doesn't make any kind of sense to worry about your health. Then there's the stench that comes with war. Dead bodies, blood, shit. A cigarette deadens your sense of smell."

She coughs once and flicks ash onto the floor.

"You may as well have a drink. We might be here a bit."

Lian looks over her shoulder at the bartender and the woman by the bar. "How do I order water in Bosnian?"

"Oh, they speak English. This bar caters to us bastards."

She crushes out her cigarette and stands up. "Right back," she says, and walks up to the bar. "Water, please."

The bartender shakes his head. "Water has to have a drink with it."

"Scotch and water, then. And a couple of bar towels, please."

He makes the drink for her, his hands and the glasses under the bar so she is unable to see what he is doing. He sets the drink on the counter and throws down a couple of bar towels, as if he knows why she has asked. She gives him a few bills and waits for him to start making change before she turns away, leaving him whatever is left. The drink is a little heavy on the scotch and light on the water.

"Sometimes I don't know what else to do," Jack says.

"About what?" she asks, and hands him the towels.

"Everything," he says, pushing the first towel between his legs. "Gray. My wife. My legs. It all seems too much. Bloody war takes everything."

"Have you seen a lot of them?"

"Yes," he says, taking another cigarette off the table. He is able to light it himself this time and takes a long drag before placing his hands on the edge of the table and looking across at Lian. "But none like the one here."

He shakes his head slowly, his eyes closed.

"I don't think I ever saw anyone come to a war looking like they already had shell shock. I thought Gray had done other kinds of war correspondence before, but then I talked to him. I had to admire him a little. Going from covering state fairs and sports to . . ." he opens his eyes and waves his cigarette in the air, "to a carnival of the insane."

She sips her drink and waits for him to continue, but his eyes are suddenly not steady. They wobble in his head and, even though his face is pointed at her, she can tell he can't see her. His hands tremble and cigarette ash flakes off, lands on the table. She reaches over and takes the cigarette from his fingers, crushes it out. Waits. When his eyes finally focus on her again, it seems as if he might cry.

"Do you ever get pains? Just pains for no reason. Like a shooting pain that comes and goes?"

"No," she says.

"I get them from time to time. Ever since I was shot. It starts in my knees and travels up to my lower back. It's like someone grinding my bones with a broken drill. I want to die sometimes." He picks up another cigarette and lights it. "Not much longer and I think we can leave," he says.

Emil stands in the shadows smoking a cigarette as he waits for Goran to return. This back alley in the dark reminds him of nightmares. There is the trickle of water on concrete. A scuttle of paper, and rats. The sound of the wind. He drops the cigarette to the ground and crushes it with his boot.

A door opens, then footsteps on the concrete. Emil presses his back against the wall. The silhouette of a person appears down the alley from him. There is the suggestion of movement, a rustle of fabric, and then the click of a lighter and the jump of flame. At first he thinks it is Goran, but as the man holds the flame to the cigarette and the glow spreads over his face, Emil can tell it is someone else.

After a moment the man drops the half-smoked cigarette on the pavement, turns, and goes back inside. Again Emil is alone in the alley, and he relaxes a little. He stiffens at the sound of the door again.

"Emil," Goran says.

Emil steps out of the shadows and hurries down the alley.

"They want to meet you," Goran says.

"What for?'

"I do not know."

Goran leads him into the building and down a wide hallway to another door. Inside the room two men sit at a low table with four plastic file boxes in front of them. They are dressed alike, in matching blue tracksuits, which makes their other similarities stand out so much Emil can almost believe they are twins. One of the two must be the man who came out for half a cigarette, but Emil can't tell which. Everyone smells of tobacco. The two men are introduced as Merhmet and Halil.

"Drink?" Merhmet asks.

"No, thank you," Emil says.

"It is quite good beer, for once."

"No, thank you."

"He might have become a little fundamental," Goran says.

Merhmet nods, holds his hands up. "I understand."

"And why are you going to Potočari?" Halil asks.

Emil glances at Goran, then back at both men. "To identify a body."

"There are a lot of bodies around there," Halil says.

"We want you to do us a favor then, in return for the car," Merhmet says, placing a tightly wrapped package on the table. "There is an associate who runs a bakery there."

Emil glances at Goran, who stands with his back turned. "That is a big favor for a car."

Halil shrugs. "For the car and a little money to help your crippled cousin."

Emil reaches into his jacket and takes out his pack of cigarettes.

"Please, no smoking inside," Merhmet says. "There is gas."

Emil turns and opens the door to leave.

"Do you not want the car then?" Halil asks.

"I need to talk to you alone," Emil says to Goran.

"We will be back," Goran tells them.

They leave the room and walk back down the hallway to the alley. Outside, Emil lights his cigarette.

"It is only heroin," Goran says. "I am only trying to put some money in your pocket, for Stjepan."

"Not this again. It is dangerous."

"You cannot tell me that you do not need money to get him home."

"I do not need money this badly."

"Listen." Goran leans close to Emil; his thin neck stretches out like a vulture's. "I would not ask you to do this if it were not an easy thing."

"Who are these guys anyway?"

"Small-time. Small-time, trying to be big. You worked for them once before you ran back to the farm. This is the first time they have had heroin."

"How do you know?"

"I am their biggest distributor, and you know how small-time I am."

"You are crazy."

Goran shrugs. "You need a car, and I know you do not have enough money to help Stjepan."

"Damn you," Emil says. "Can you not get a legitimate car?"

"Have I ever been legitimate? You came to me because you need a car now. If you wanted a legitimate car you could have asked Katja to help you rent one from the hotel, or bought one."

"You know I cannot afford to buy one. And Katja would not help with this."

"Did you ask?"

Emil frowns, kicks at the concrete.

"See, that is why I have given you a car that will pay you."

Emil looks up at the slip of night sky coming down between the crumbling buildings. This is one of the reasons he never likes coming to the city. The worst parts of it always seem to find him if he stays more than a day. He tries to think of any other way to get his hands on a car for little or no money, but he knows his own desperation would cause him to pick badly. He would be caught if he tried to steal one.

"How do they have an associate in Potočari? There are no Muslims there anymore."

"They are equal-opportunity pushers."

"So their contact is a Serb."

"Yes."

"I guess I do not mind delivering heroin to a Serb if he is going to sell it to other Serbs."

"You want revenge too much."

"And you will forgive anything for money," Emil says.

"I have a big heart," Goran says.

"Odi u kurac," Emil says.

"I even forgive you."

"If anything happens I will not be so generous."

"Nothing will happen, Emil. Nothing that you do not bring upon yourself."

"What if I am unable to make the delivery?"

Goran shrugs. "One of us will have to pay them."

"You will."

"And then you will pay me."

"After this you and I are over."

Goran nods. "I always had a feeling that peace would make us enemies."

Lian helps Jack to his room and leaves him sprawled on the bed while she runs water in the bathtub for him. He is asleep when she comes out of the bathroom, and she has to shake him awake.

"Go take a bath," she says.

"Yes, of course. Will you stay and keep an eye on me a little longer?"

"Yes." She sits on the bed while he goes into the bathroom. He leaves the door open a bit and talks to her through the gap.

"I think Gray had a way of sneaking up on people," Jack says. "One moment I was thinking, *A bloody rookie,* but then I was looking for him in the lobby every morning to see where he was going to go. He had charisma."

"He was honest," Lian says.

"Yes, but that's not all of it. He was like some kind of magnet."

"Yes, he was," she says.

"He would get an idea sometimes, and you couldn't help but go along."

Lian squeezes her eyes shut and presses her hands to her face. She wishes Jack would shut up.

I would like to see you this weekend. On the phone, Gray's voice always sounded higher than it did in person.

But I might have plans, she said.

Might have plans? You're not sure?

Well, no.

Then make plans with me so that you will have plans.

Gray.

What?

Nothing. Fine. What do you want to do?

Do you like amusement parks?

What kind of question is that?

He laughed. *It's a loaded question. I don't know. Do you?*

I don't hate them.

Okay, Worlds of Fun. We'll ride some roller coasters, things like that.

I've never been on a roller coaster.

You're kidding me.

No.

We'll start slow then.

She doesn't remember all they did that weekend. What she does remember clearly is the way her body trembled when she stepped off the first roller coaster and the easy way his arm slid around her waist to steady her. Something opened inside her, a window looking onto a larger vista. When she stopped trembling he took his arm away, and that vista shrank away to nothing. She took his hand then, and the feeling made her brave.

Jack steps out of the bathroom, a robe wrapped tightly around him, and steadies himself with a hand against the wall. "I think the warm water loosened up the legs a little."

"Good."

"Have you been crying?"

"A little. I was thinking of Gray."

He shakes his head and limps to the bed, sits down next to her. "Emil has never told me what happened out there. I don't think he ever will. All he's said is that they got separated. I think there's more, but I won't force it out of him."

"Would he tell me?"

"You can try."

"I didn't follow anything about the war, just Gray's letters, and when they stopped I figured it was because he finally gave up on me."

"War is hell on the postal service."

"Was he upset that I didn't write back?"

"I don't think so."

She rubs her eyes and wipes the dampness on her pant legs. "I'm tired, and I think it's time I head off to my room."

"Yes, good-night."

She stands up. "Thank you."

"Thank me? No, you helped me home tonight. I should thank you. I only wish you hadn't seen me like that."

"Good-night, Jack," she says and leaves his room.

In Pursuit

The hospital is small, and Emil hates it. It is a dumping ground for the wounded who have no other place to go, or those who are too damaged to be cared for by what is left of their families. He steps through the entrance and is assaulted by the antiseptic smell that he associates now with hopelessness. With regret. The walls hold their echoes close, as if the sounds that were with him on the sidewalk have come here to die too.

He pushes through a set of doors at the back of the lobby, then climbs a wide flight of stairs to the top floor. He won't take the elevator and avoids the places where he might encounter patients.

The boy's room faces away from the sunrise and, with the curtains shut, holds the last of the night's darkness. Emil slips into the dimness and goes to the foot of Stjepan's bed, tries not to look at the flat place where his left arm should be or the contorted form his withered, lifeless legs have taken in the night. Emil takes in a deep breath to calm himself and waits.

"Who is it?"

"Emil."

"Have you come to take me home?"

"I am sorry, Stjepan, not yet. The house is not ready."

"I do not like this place, Emil."

"I know," he says and comes around the bed to stand beside the boy. He takes Stjepan's hand, squeezes the cold fingers.

"Katja came to see me yesterday, or the day before. It is hard to remember."

"What did you talk about?"

"She read to me. A book from England, I think, but it was set in India."

This close to him, even in the faint light, Emil can see the smaller damages to the boy's body. The left side of his face creased and made uneven by pink scar tissue. His empty eye sockets. Emil looks away, through a small gap between the curtains at the brightening sky.

"Katja said you are finally looking for Gray."

"Yes."

"And the woman in Gray's photograph? She is here?"

"Yes."

"I remember the pictures. Is she as pretty as the pictures?"

"She is older, but yes."

"Is she here with us now?"

"No, it is just us two."

"Good. I would not want her to see me."

"I understand."

"If you find Gray and he is alive, tell him he has a promise to keep."

"And if he is not alive?"

"It does not matter then."

"What did he promise?"

"It is a secret. And you could not do it."

Emil frowns, tries to keep his frustration from exposing itself when he speaks. He walks away from the bed and opens the curtains so he can see the sky and the jagged contours of the city lit up by the sunrise. The windows can't be opened, but he imagines he can hear the first faint voices calling the faithful to prayer.

"You know he disappeared at Potočari. He is most likely dead."

"Why are you looking for him then? Why did you have the woman come to help you?"

"I have to make sure he gets home."

"And after him, me?"

"Yes."

"They say there are ghosts in the woods around Potočari and Srebrenica."

"I have heard." Emil turns back to the boy and touches the smoother side of his face. "I must be going."

"Your visits are too short."

"I am sorry, Stjepan. When I get back, we will go home."

"Promise?" Stjepan asks, his face still moving as if his eyes are there to express his hope.

"Promise," Emil says. He goes to the door, stops, and looks back at the boy. The secret Stjepan mentioned is obvious to Emil, and Stjepan is right. It is something Emil could not bring himself to do.

Lian hates this waiting. The stasis of the last day has given her time to think. Time to doubt again. But it would be pointless to turn around now, go home to Daniel, and resume that life. All the questions she had convinced him to stop asking would return, especially now, after the phone call. As she climbs down the main stairs to the lobby, she looks to be sure Jack is still sitting by the front windows. The sunlight falls through on him, and he seems pale and transparent. She goes across the lobby and sits in a chair facing him.

"How are your legs today?"

"Fine," he says.

She can tell he doesn't want to talk about it.

"You know," he says, "the more I think about it, the more I think Gray might actually be alive."

"What do you mean?"

He presses his lips together as if trying to make a decision about what he will say. "There are some things I've been meaning to tell you, but haven't been sure how. They might be hard to hear."

"Well, tell me and I'll deal with it."

"When Gray first arrived, there was a French TV reporter named Suzzette Boisson. She attached herself to him. A little wartime romance, I believe. She was only here a few months before her cameraman was killed one day, and she left."

Lian sits back in her chair and looks out the window at the street. She feels like water flowing down a drain.

"I guess what I'm saying," Jack says, "is that, after they were separated, he could have thought Emil was dead and simply taken off for France. Emil tried contacting her, but she's not written back yet."

"Jack," she says, "are you speculating for yourself? Or are you trying to get me to go home?"

"I'm trying to prepare you for some potentially very bad news."

"It doesn't matter anyway."

"Maybe none of this matters. I have no idea what happened out there. I've never gotten Emil to tell me the whole story. Maybe I'm just trying to feel important. Excuse me."

Jack gets up from his chair, leans heavily on his cane, then moves off across the lobby in the direction of the restrooms.

Lian is surprised at how easily she can imagine Gray with someone else. How she can imagine the way he might touch another woman's hair after kissing her, where he would place his hands after undressing her. She hates how it suddenly makes her body feel sucked into the chair. Her weight centered and heavy on the cushion.

When Jack returns, he eases himself into his chair and sighs.

"What was he like with her?" she asks.

"If someone like her had treated me the way she treated Gray, well," Jack reaches inside his coat for his flask, "I once married that woman."

"Jack," she says, "it's early for that."

He looks down at the flask. "I do suppose so," he says and screws the top back on.

"So you think that means he went to her if he survived?"

"No. It was your picture he always carried. If he had a picture of her, I never saw it."

They sit quietly, looking out the window at the street. A few cars pass by. Pedestrians trickle along the sidewalk.

"Why, if you don't mind me asking, did you and Gray . . . come apart?"

Lian looks down at her hands, knits her fingers together, unknits them, then presses them under her thighs. "I married someone else."

Jack nods, takes out his pack of cigarettes. "Yes, but what was the real reason? Did you think he had a fetish for Asian women?"

She is silent and still for a moment. "I don't know."

"Did you ask him? It seems like the simplest thing to do."

"Jack," Lian says, "I already feel awful. I've felt awful for years, and I—"

He raises his hands. "Sorry to push. It's hard not to be a journalist sometimes."

Lian lets herself sink deeper into the chair. She watches Jack put the unlit cigarette in his mouth, then take it out and stuff it back in the pack.

"I never asked him," she finally says. "I was only worried when he wasn't around."

It is nearly noon when Emil parks the Mercedes across the street from the hotel. He watches Jack and Lian rise from their seats by the window and walk across the lobby to the stairs. It will be a few more minutes before they return with their bags. He reaches under the driver's seat and makes sure the package is firmly wedged in place. It is not the safest hiding place, but he doesn't plan to keep it very long.

He gets out of the car and opens the trunk, then waits for Jack and Lian to come out of the hotel. From where he stands, he can see the hills and, for a moment, feels crosshairs on him. The tingle of panic under the skin of his hands.

Jack and Lian push open the doors and step onto the sidewalk, pause for a truck to pass, then come across the street. Emil takes their bags and packs them into the trunk. Jack takes the backseat so he can stretch out his legs, and Lian sits up front.

"How hot is this car?" Jack asks.

"It is not stolen." Emil turns the ignition and revs the engine against Jack's laughter.

"What is there to listen to?" Lian reaches to turn the knobs on the radio.

"Nothing. It does not work."

Lian sits back in her seat, pulls her long hair over her shoulder. "Great."

Emil drives them out of the city. Only the rumble of the engine fills the air between them.

The lift and drop of the elevator make Daniel feel the sleep he has been fighting off. The doors open, and he steps out. It's as if he is stumbling through fog on his way down the hall to his room. The lock is stubborn against his key. In the room, the light is hazy gray. He sets down his bags, then turns on the lamp. He wants to begin looking for Lian but can't imagine taking any more steps than the ones that carry him to the bed. He lies down and falls asleep.

When he wakes up the next morning, he feels covered in cobwebs. There is a faint light through the gaps in the curtains, and the sound of cars. Slowly he undresses and steps into the bathroom to shower, still peeling the sleep off his brain, still sifting through memories.

He watched her through the clear shower curtain as she put her hands under the spray of water, then pressed them to her face. Slowly hidden by mist.

How long are you planning to be gone? he asked.

A week or so.

I don't see why you insist on going alone.

It's just a business trip.

Why do I think you're not telling me everything?

She was silent for a moment. The form of her body completely blurred behind the shower curtain.

I don't know, Daniel. Why?

Because . . . he started but was unable to finish. Finally, with the steam thick around him, his image in the mirror nothing but a smudge, he left the bathroom.

Should he have said it was because she refused to be herself anymore? Or was it because of other, smaller things? There were times he had seen her sniffing at things like an animal. She had tampered with the scent of his clothes, changed soaps and detergents and fabric softeners until he was sometimes confused by his own smell. He couldn't think of a way to ask her about those things, or a way to say, *Yes, this is what makes me suspicious.* His need to trust her always at war with the questions about her silences. After her phone call from Bosnia he thought he knew how madness would feel.

As he dresses, his mind pulls itself from its fog, although he still feels tired. He picks up the picture of Lian he brought with him.

He doesn't know the name of the hotel she called him from, doesn't know if she is alone, or with others. All of the things he doesn't know pile up in his mind. For a moment he considers himself as he stands in this hotel room in another country with a picture of his wife in his hand and no idea where she might be. He tries to decide if he is being foolish or if rushing to the airport and spending so much money to fly here has any justification. How do these actions define him now? Concerned loved one? Jealous husband? Desperate man?

He wants her home. He wants the truth from her, finally.

Katja is sweeping the entrance to the restaurant and sees an Asian man leave the elevator and go to the front desk. He takes a picture from his shirt pocket and shows it to the young man working there. She wonders briefly who this person is looking for, but there are so many people searching through this country now. She puts away her broom and dustpan, then goes to the back table of the restaurant, near the kitchen doors, and begins wrapping silverware in paper napkins, closing the sticky ends of a paper band around the bundle.

This is her favorite part of the shift, sitting at a back table carefully wrapping silverware. Since the end of the war, since Emil's refusal to come back to Sarajevo, she has looked for moments of careful repetition. She wakes in the morning to one cup of coffee and a little milk on the days she goes to the temporary school in her *mahala* to teach history. She waits tables at the Holiday Inn in the evenings on those days. On Saturday and Sunday she works early at the hotel. The teaching for her heart, the hotel for her pocketbook.

She looks up from the table again to see the Asian man coming into the restaurant. He takes a seat at a table in her section, as far from the other three guests as he can get. She slides out of the booth and walks to the man's table.

He orders a soda and a sandwich. Katja writes the order down, glances at the photograph he has laid face down on the table by his elbow. He doesn't seem to notice her still standing there as he copies the names of hotels from the front desk's city guide onto a small piece of paper. He doesn't even look up when she says she'll return in a moment with his drink. By the time she takes his food to him there is a crowd in the restaurant, and she is too busy to be curious.

They spent the night in the car, parked along the road with a few other travelers. Their journey delayed by a detour around a bridge under repair. Now, in the cool, overcast morning, Lian sits on the ground beside the road and waits for Jack to return from the cluster of trees a few yards away. She tries to ignore the subtle vibration in the center of her chest. Gray could be around the next turn in the road, and she is no longer sure she wants to know he is really dead. It's too late now to go back to her chosen blindness with Daniel.

"Tell me about Gray," she says to Emil. "Tell me what you did after Sarajevo."

"It is a boring story," he says. "Until Jack was shot."

"I want to hear it."

"We went to Travnik." He shrugs. "We took a lot of pictures of horrible things. We drank a lot and talked."

"What did you talk about?"

"Sometimes we would get drunk and talk about things the way people talk about history."

"Was this when Mrs. Bašić met him?"

"Almost. The town she lived in was occupied by the Serbs when we first arrived."

"And she was there? In Travnik?"

"No, she stayed in her home. Her family is Eastern Orthodox, so they left her alone even though she spoke out against the Serbs."

"Oh," she says.

Emil sits down next to her. "Gray and I talked about many things, but he did not talk much about you unless I asked him questions and he was drunk."

"What did you ask him?"

"I asked him why he did not try to win you back, and he always said the choice was not his."

Lian looks away from him, up at the empty blue sky.

"The choice never seemed to be mine either," she says.

She pulls at the edges of her memory for something else about him, something that will center her perception of him against the one Jack and Emil have given her. It feels as if Gray has become a shadow. Years ago he had been as solid to her as stone, his body next to hers inevitable, demanding her attention.

I've been thinking about you.

Really?

You seem surprised.

What were you thinking? she asked.

I was thinking you could come with me while I do this thing at this restaurant.

There were undone things at work. There were meetings to attend. There were mock-ups to review. The new brochure was behind schedule. She left it all to meet him and was puzzled that he didn't have his camera.

What's the thing you need to do?

See you.

She understands now that he was teaching her to accept the pieces of him that didn't make sense. Back then those things were small shards of rock with single letters carved in them, one letter of an entire alphabet she didn't have. She would have walked away then if she could. If the simple touch of his fingers on the back of her wrist hadn't felt like a conversation. If he hadn't helped her be brave in the dark.

Back in the car, with Emil driving them slowly through the hills toward Potočari, she rests her head against the seat and stares at the hills until she is no longer aware of them, the horizon slipping out of focus in her half sleep. The vibrations of the car on the road are hypnotic, passing her into daydreams of finding Gray that arrive disconnected from logic. The flight of a dove over water opens a door in a basement, and Gray falls through like lightning. There, a stone again in her mind.

At the Europa Hotel, the last hotel Daniel is going to check this day, the clerk tells him the woman had been there and left the day before, the day Daniel arrived.

"Did she say where she was going?"

"No."

"Who was she with?"

"An old man with a cane and another man. A Bosnian. They got in a car and left."

Daniel thanks him and walks out the front door and onto the sidewalk. The light is beginning to fade, pale blue swirling into reds and oranges, then black off to the east of the city. Night drags itself into the sky. He starts back to the Holiday Inn. The people on the streets with him pass through shadows, then through light, then through shadows again. They register in his consciousness the way fragments of architecture are looked at but not seen.

An old man with a cane? Another man, a Bosnian? Neither of them, he is sure, is the man in the photograph, and unless she has lied to him a great deal, he is certain she has never been to this part of the world before.

Until the night of their wedding, he thought he knew as much about her as he could. Then the scar and its revelation of an undisclosed history. So many times after that night he lay awake in their bed, staring at her shoulder while she slept. He wanted to wake her each time, force an answer out of her. He knows the connection is there, the Caucasian man in the photograph, the scar on her shoulder, but there is no proof. Only his speculation. His intuition.

When he returns to the Holiday Inn, he is hungry. He takes the same table he had earlier that day and lays the photograph in front of him. Her face, the placid stare directed at the world, leaps across the time between then and now. The look is foreign to the Lian he has known for the last few years. What it is, he decides, is the Lian he first met. The woman he fell in love with and whose return he has been awaiting.

Daniel arrived on time on the appointed Sunday five years earlier. His small gift, a handmade teapot for Mrs. Jiang, to show gratitude for being invited to their home, was delivered with a slight bow as he entered the living room. He hoped it would show a good mix of tradition and modernity. He shook hands with Dr. Jiang.

My daughters are always late. Come, I will introduce you to my son. Dr. Jiang led Daniel out of the living room and down a dark hallway. One of the bedrooms had been turned into an office. Inside, a small desk stood by the window, its top nearly empty except for a single banker's lamp on the right corner. The polished shade reflected the light coming through the window. A sparkle of green.

Dr. Jiang introduced him to David, and from the way David sat in the chair at the desk, then rose to shake hands, Daniel decided he disliked him.

David is in medical school now, Dr. Jiang said.

A house full of doctors, Daniel said.

My sisters are not doctors, David told him. *They do other things.*

Like what?

David shrugged, and Daniel wondered if it meant he didn't care, didn't know, or both.

Lian is in business, Dr. Jiang said, *but Kay is a doctor.*

Kay is a veterinarian, which isn't a real doctor, David said.

There are vets I'd trust more than some surgeons, Daniel said.

Whether Dr. Jiang agreed or disagreed with his son was impossible to tell. He went to look out the window, and Daniel could not see his face. After a few moments of tense silence, while he wondered if there was anything else he could say to Dr. Jiang or his son, Dr. Jiang finally turned away from the window and smiled at him.

They are here, he said.

David rolled his eyes and stood up. Father and son walked together down the hall, and Daniel followed them. He wondered if accepting this offer had been a good idea. Dr. Jiang had talked about his daughters quite a bit, but they had not been the reason he'd accepted the dinner invitation. Dr. Jiang was important at the hospital, and although Daniel wasn't too concerned about upward mobility, he had seen the invitation as a sign of respect. Something he would not jeopardize.

Dr. Jiang's two daughters came through the front door as Daniel entered the living room. He was introduced to them quickly, as if they had other things to do and other places to be. Kay had her black hair cut short and was nearly as tall as Daniel. She didn't smile at him and disappeared into the kitchen. Lian was a little shorter than Kay. She smiled at him, then briefly shook his hand. Daniel was led into the dining room by Dr. Jiang and seated across the table from Lian. As the dinner progressed, Daniel could pick out the birth order of the three children. Kay had been first, then Lian, and finally David. Lian spoke little that night. When she caught him looking at her, the amused, even expression slid into place. He felt as if he were an insect being studied.

When Dr. Jiang invited him to the next Sunday dinner, he accepted only because he wished to study Lian's expression again. He was curious about her silence, the reason why she seemed to smile to herself when nothing funny had been said and she thought no one was looking.

"Would you like to order now?"

Daniel looks up from the table at the waitress who helped him that morning. "Have you been working all day?"

"No," she says. "A split shift."

"Of course," he says, and slides the photograph he'd been staring at off the menu and looks over the listings.

"This woman seems familiar," the waitress says. "Oh, yes."

"You have seen her?" He reacts, even against the will to remain calm, and pushes up from the bench. His movement abbreviated by the presence of the table.

"No. Just in photographs. But I knew that man."

Daniel watches her hand, the lazy gesture to the blurred image of the man behind Lian. He drops into the seat again, his strength to stand draining away.

"Who is he?"

The woman hesitates, and for a moment Daniel is afraid she won't tell him.

"Please, she's my wife and I'm trying to find her."

The woman looks around the restaurant. Daniel looks as well, wondering what she might be afraid of. There are two American soldiers at a table on the far side. There are a few other official-looking people in suits. No one important to him, no one who might be interested. She finally slides into the booth with Daniel.

"I knew Gray during the war when my boyfriend, Emil, worked as his interpreter."

You should *stay here tonight,* Emil said.

The attack was concentrated somewhere to the east. Artillery and mortar rounds crashed into the city. In the beginning of the war, Katja had hurried to the basement of her apartment building at the start of each attack. Now she hardly moved unless the attack was in her part of the city. She had become an expert at guessing the caliber of shells falling on them by the sounds they made in the air.

Katja watched the American set down his camera bag and return to the small circle of light where she sat with Emil and Stjepan. She had seen him a few times at the Holiday Inn, but in the shadows she was afraid of him. He was more gaunt than Emil.

We have a little šlivo, Emil said.

And I've got cigarettes, the American said.

Outside their circle of light, the city was beaten. The boom of artillery and machine guns like an erratic drumbeat. They sat around the small firebox, occasionally stopping their conversation to listen to the shelling when its voice grew louder than their own. A few candle stubs burned in old saucers that caught the dripping wax so new candles could be made. They drank *šlivo* from tin mugs. The American cigarettes were passed around, even to Stjepan, and they talked. Told rumors of the war.

The fighting receded after two in the morning. The hour and the drink tugged Emil and Stjepan down to sleep, but Katja lay awake and watched Gray smoke. He lay on his back, his head resting on his bunched-up jacket. There were only the last two candles and their tiny, faint circles of orange light and the red dot of his cigarette to illuminate the room. She watched him take a photograph out of his camera bag and angle it toward the nearest candle. Inside the glowing circle she could tell it was the photograph of a woman.

Is she your wife? Katja whispered.

No.

May I see it closer?

He handed the picture to her, and she turned it to the light.

She is very beautiful, Katja said. After a moment more, she handed the photo back to Gray.

He slipped it into his camera bag and crushed out his cigarette. It seemed like he was going to sleep, but he turned on his side and looked at her. He offered her a cigarette, which she took, then he took another for himself.

She hurt me very badly, he said.

You were in love with her?

Very much.

How long ago?

Almost two years ago. I guess I'm still in love with her.

Then why are you here?

He smiled as if he'd been asked the same question many times. It was the smile of someone resigned to a miserable fate. *I'm here to kill her memory.*

Or kill yourself?

Yes.

She did not know what to say to him then, and they remained silent until she had finished her cigarette and dropped the butt into the black firebox.

Good-night, she said.

Yes, good-night, he said and lit another cigarette off the butt of the first.

"***Where did*** they go?"

Katja looks around the empty restaurant again. Her shift ended an hour ago, and she wants to go home, but this man seems desperate for anything she has to say. Almost as desperate to listen to her as she has been desperate to talk.

"They are going to Potočari to look for Gray's remains."

"Where is that?"

"Northeast of here. It was part of the Srebrenica Safe Area."

He picks up his photograph and stands up from the booth. "Thank you," he says.

"Are you leaving now?"

"In the morning," he says. "I'll need to rent a car."

She smiles at him. "I wish you luck."

"Thank you, Katja," he says and leaves.

Later Katja walks home, avoiding the bright pools the streetlights make as they come on. She wonders if she should ask to go with Daniel. He hasn't offered, but she doesn't think he would turn down the company, and she is certain he could use an interpreter. It wouldn't be for too many days, and she should try to get out of the city, if only for a short time, to break the monotony.

Waiting for Emil to make up his mind could go on forever, she thinks. There is not a body he can bury, and Emil needs to bury things before he can move away from them. She could see that in the way he clung to his family's house, to the memory of his dead fiancée. There is no way to bury a whole house. No way to bury memories without evidence that they won't walk through the door tomorrow.

At home Katja leaves the lights off, navigates her possessions by the dim light sifting like dust through the closed blinds. She tells herself she needs to be more patient with Emil. Eventually he will have to admit the truth. It is sad, she thinks, that he has had to wait. She got word of her fiancé's death almost immediately after the war ended. Her mother came all the way from Bihać to look for her. She brought news of the family and that Petar had been killed defending the city.

Only Stjepan was left of Emil's family.

What she could never understand was why he thought he had to wait at the farm for Mira to come back, or to learn of her death. Of course she is sure Emil doesn't understand why she wants to stay in the city. Gravity maybe. The weight of history. When she found out Petar was dead, she did not want to return to Bihać, even to be with her family after years of being separated by their respective sieges. She wanted to stay away from the town and what was left of Petar's family. Maybe it was that she had embarked on a romance before knowing what might have happened. Maybe she didn't want to navigate those avenues and familiar places again, or feel guilty for being alive. Emil, however, seems to want to dive into the center of his scars.

Daniel now has a name for the unfocused face behind Lian. He had hoped *Gray Banick* would seem familiar when he finally heard it, that there would be something like recognition, but there is none of that. The name is without any meaning outside its connection to this face in the photograph.

He sits at the small table in his room, staring out the window at the city. Maybe she will come back. Maybe he only needs to be patient. To be without her is something he doesn't want to consider, and he doesn't know how to sort the feelings he has. There is only the need to find her, desperate enough he has traveled here to purge this loss of equilibrium. To let her go like this, to a shadow, would be disgraceful.

He gets up from the chair and turns off the light, but in the dark there is nothing to distract him. He returns to the table to sit and stare at the lights of the city.

It has become difficult for Stjepan to tell the difference between his waking memories and his dreams. Sometimes it is only the sound of a voice or the nurse's cool hands on his chest that let him know he is awake. He swings back and forth between the two worlds so easily now, guessing the time of day by the noises around him, what they feed him. Sometimes he thinks of Gray. He remembers the last night Gray stayed with them in Emil's apartment. After everyone had gone to sleep, Stjepan went and crouched next to Gray and stared at him in the dim light.

Are you awake?

Yes.

May I speak with you?

Yes.

Come with me, it is private.

He led Gray into another room of the apartment, their bodies reduced to shadows and whispers.

I am joining the army, he said.

I have heard.

It is not something I am doing because I think I will be a hero.

I understand.

But there is something I am afraid of. Have you seen the wounded, the bad ones?

Yes.

I do not want to live like that. If I am wounded badly, will you . . . finish me?

Gray was silent, and Stjepan was afraid he would say no.

Are you certain?

Yes. If I must always be cared for, I do not want to live.

I will do what I can.

Now there is no hope for that. When he thinks of that night, of Gray's promise, he doesn't hate Gray for his failure. The years of the war taught Stjepan again and again that the ruler of the universe is chance. Plans could be made, but they should never be depended upon. Now he is left only with the hope that someday Emil will take him home and somehow, in that place, he can find a way to finish this life.

Hungry for images, he returns in his mind to the day he should have died. He woke before Katja and ate a few pieces of bread in the dark. Then he left. Emil and Gray had been gone for months. The last news he'd heard of them had come when Jack MacKenzie had been wounded near Travnik.

The war was grinding down. The Americans and the United Nations were finally doing something, even though what they did was mostly useless. The day-to-day never changed, but Stjepan saw that the Bosnian Army was making progress in places. They had all heard news of gains around Bihać and that the army would link up a corridor with the central part of the country. Good news after the time, months earlier, when it seemed the pocket around Bihać would fall to a coup from within the Bosnian ranks.

That day he took a rifle and ammunition from a man, the clarity of his face lost now, and Stjepan can't tell if it is a trick of his imagination or if the man had been wounded, his face smeared out of focus by a bullet or an explosion. Stjepan was the youngest in his team, not yet sixteen, but he was not the youngest fighter in the army. There were thirteen-year-olds and fourteen-year-olds, their bodies not much longer than the rifles they carried to the front trenches.

As they walked to the post they were to relieve, the sun rose and warmed Stjepan's face. He carried his rifle across his shoulders and trailed behind the four other fighters. He remembers the moment when the feeling started in his stomach. As he passed a small building where they turned to enter the trenches they would follow to the farthest outpost, his belly seemed to shrink and pull up tight against his heart.

A girl, roughly his age, stood in the sunlight cast against a building. She stood, now in his memory, flat against the wall. Her arms were held out, palms against the rough surface behind her. A breeze pressed the tan material of her dress tight against her body, and she looked at him. Strands of brown hair slipped across her face. Her large brown eyes. A smile.

It seemed she was the cause of the feeling in his stomach. A pretty girl, standing where only sunlight could touch her, looking at him and smiling. He stared at her over his left shoulder, thought for a moment he could run to her and get her name, promise to meet her that night. He thought she might kiss him, might let him put his hand on one of her long thighs. He stared at her, studied the gentle, emerging curves of her slender body, and imagined she would move like a reed when she stepped away from the wall.

She is an angel, he thought as the white light and the heat swirled around him. Then, before the light snapped out to black, she screamed.

A mortar round. That was what he was told by some doctor he could not see. *We could not save your arm or your eyes. They were too badly burned.*

He didn't believe what he had lost until he was able to touch the stump where his left arm abruptly ended above the elbow.

My legs?

I'm sorry, you are paralyzed from the waist down. A piece of shrapnel nicked your spine above the hip.

There are times, swirling in and out of his two worlds, when he still feels everything he lost. He imagines raising his left arm to his face, expecting his own fingers to touch his lips, to see his own hands appear out of the blackness, but the sensation, like the solidity of mist, dissolves.

Now he waits for the voices and the cool hands, stretches out his hearing for the footsteps in the hallway, the rolling wave of voices coming down to his room every day. The nurses stay with him longest when he is moved into a wheelchair so he can be fed, so his sheets can be changed. There are two. A man and a woman most times. The man to lift him and carry him to the chair. The woman who feeds him, talks to him with her gentle voice. He imagines it is the girl he saw against the wall that day.

Will they be coming to take me home today? he asks her every day.

I have not heard.

Tell me what it is like outside, he says to her.

The sun is out, and there are birds singing.

I cannot hear them.

The windows are closed.

I would like to go outside today, he says.

I will see if that can be arranged.

On the days when he is taken outside, he turns his blind face toward the heat of the sun. As he is wheeled around, he reaches his hand out for things that will tell him where he is in the world. He imagines they take him to a walled, private garden. He smells flowers he has never known the names of, but his hand only ever touches things rough and hard. Things that could be brick or concrete. The flowers held away from his path.

Not sure if he is sleeping or awake, he senses someone in his room. The faint draw of breath. The displacement of air by the movement of a body. He wonders if it is Emil, or Katja, and if maybe they have come to take him home, but he hopes only enough to keep himself from slipping completely out of reality.

There have been times when he has convinced himself that if Emil would only say they were going home, it would be enough to stop his heart. And that, in the end, is what he wants more. Even though he can speak and hear, can touch the things around him, he cannot imagine much of a life he could live.

The sound of breath again, as if it is coming painfully.

"Are you not going to say hello?" Stjepan asks.

There are warm hands on his face. A man's hands.

"Is it time to change the sheets?"

The owner of the hands does not speak, but his breathing changes, seems to halt somewhere in the middle of his presence. Stjepan reaches up and touches the man's arm, moves his hand up to the shoulder, the neck, and finally the man's face. His cheeks are wet.

"Do I know you?"

With his hand on the man's cheek, he is able to feel him nod.

"I am blind, you know. It would be better if you spoke."

The man leans down over him. Stjepan can feel the heat of his whole body now, the movement of the man's breath on his cheek, then against his ear. The whispered voice has an accent, the Bosnian words slightly mispronounced. "I am sorry it has been so long."

"I forgive you," Stjepan says. A tightness forms in his head. His body sending messages to tear ducts he no longer has. There is only the heavy wrenching of his chest and the gusts of air from his lungs. He knows the warm hands that hold his face for a moment longer, then disappear and come back to touch his arm. The contact soothes him, and slowly he is able to catch his breath.

"Emil is looking for you," Stjepan says. "The woman in the photograph has come to help him. We all thought you were dead."

"It does not matter. I have a promise to keep. Do you want me to keep my promise or wait?"

"How will you do it?"

"Morphine."

"Will you stay with me?"

"Yes."

"Do not wait."

"You will need an interpreter, unless you can speak the language."

Daniel looks up from his breakfast. She is not dressed for work, and she has a bag slung over her shoulder, a cardboard box in her arms. He can see she has been crying. Her eyes are wet and red. She sits down across from him in the booth.

"You want to come along with me?"

"Yes," she says. "I need to find Emil."

Daniel doesn't want to pry any deeper. If she wishes to tell him, he will listen. He's never been good at getting things out of people who don't want to tell, unless they are patients. With Lian, he gave up trying. It has always been easier to be more like his parents than like his white friends. No dwelling on emotions, just taking care of responsibilities. Paying the bills. Having children and sending them to school. There were never moments like this. He watches Katja as she rubs her eyes and aggravates the redness.

"I don't speak the language. Thank you. The people at the rental place said it is dangerous to go there alone. Will you be able to leave soon?"

"Yes," she says. "There is nothing left here."

He pushes away his plate, not sure how to respond to such a cryptic comment.

"Stjepan has died," she says.

For a moment the name doesn't register with Daniel. His mind flips down through memory until he recollects the story she told him. "I'm sorry," he says.

"Thank you."

He reaches across the table and touches her cold hand. A gesture, he hopes, that will show the empathy he is trying hard to find.

Through a Field of Ghosts, 1993–1994

Jack watched as Gray climbed into the back of the Land Rover and fished a cigarette out of the pack tucked in his shirt pocket. It was hard to remember what Gray had been like a few months ago. Whether his cool, detached demeanor had been present all the time was something Jack couldn't sort out. Had it been there all along, or was it only more pronounced now that the Boisson woman was gone? It seemed as if Gray was even more casual about the war than Jack.

"There will be a thing tonight, I think," Jack said.

"A thing?"

"A little get-together. Lots of drinking and the sort. Some of the boys around here think we need to get a little out of our heads what with it being so close to the holidays."

"I'll think about it."

"Do you some good."

"Maybe."

Jack climbed into the passenger seat next to his driver. "Ready to go?"

"I suppose so," Gray said.

"Don't act so thrilled," he said and slapped Dzevad on the shoulder. "It's only the second-worst job in the world."

Jack had become unconcerned with the way driving was done in Sarajevo. Barely noticed the stops and starts, the sudden bursts of speed. A sniper was as likely to shoot at a moving vehicle as anything else on the street. With cars, the results were more dramatic. Jack had wrecked the truck a few times after being shot at. The bullet holes in the green body were like badges of rank. He had more than anyone else in the press corps. Finally, six weeks ago, he had broken down and hired Dzevad, a Bosnian who'd been a taxi driver before the war and knew the city better than he did.

Jack turned to look back at Gray from time to time. The way Gray slouched against the seat and let his head tilt back made it seem as if he had fallen asleep.

"I almost hate the quiet days," Jack said. "Would you like the rest of the day off, Dzevad?"

"I would only go home and sleep with my wife," he said.

"You make it sound bloody awful." Jack laughed.

"Yes, save me from that misery."

"Can't be that bad, can it?"

"You have not seen my wife."

Jack laughed, then turned to look out the passenger-side window. There was no view but the brick and concrete walls of the buildings lining the narrow alley they drove down. Jack rolled down the window, shivered a bit at the cold wind, then tilted his head out a little and looked up at the sky. It was peaceful for a moment, then he heard the pitch of the motor change. They were speeding up.

"Get your head back in the truck, Jack," Gray said.

That night Jack climbed the dark stairs to the third floor. Gray's room was at the far end, and he picked his way down the hall, stepped over broken furniture that had been stacked along the way. He knocked twice on the door. Gray appeared with a stack of playing cards in one hand, a cigarette in his mouth, the room behind him golden with candlelight.

"Hey, Jack."

"Thought I'd see if you were going to put in an appearance downstairs."

"No, sorry. A little too loud for me tonight. You want to come in?"

"Looks like you've got something going on in there," he said, pointing to the cards.

"Playing solitaire."

Inside the room, like all the others, the mattresses were leaning against the windows and candles burned on the table and nightstand. Gray had a halogen lantern on the table as well, its light dimmed. There were no chairs in the room, so they sat on the floor.

"I've got a couple bottles of," Gray snapped his fingers, "*šlivo?* Is that what they call it?"

"Something like that. Plum brandy."

"Kind of like it," Gray said and collected the rows of cards off the floor. "Play a little cigarette poker?"

"No. I have a feeling I'd lose all of my cigarettes and have to keep asking for them back."

Gray laughed. "A drink then?"

"Please."

Gray got up and went to one of his bags. He unpacked a few things and dropped them on the bed, then removed two collapsible plastic cups. He gave one to Jack, then went into the bathroom and came out with a bottle of the plum brandy. After he'd filled Jack's cup, he went back to the bag and began to repack it.

"Well, you are, at least, efficient," Jack said.

"Retentive."

Jack looked at the things on the bed that Gray was carefully repacking. A three-ring binder with a photograph trapped under the plastic cover caught his attention, and he picked it up before Gray repacked it. The picture was of an Asian woman, her face turned toward the camera, her body seeming to turn in another direction. Her mouth was slightly open, giving her a surprised look. Strands of hair ran across her cheeks. It had the effect of constant motion toward and away from the camera.

When Jack looked up from the picture, Gray was standing there with a cup of brandy in his hand. His eyes seemed pointed in the direction of the binder, but he had the same look on his face he had in the mornings. Distant, absorbed.

"Did you take this picture?" Jack asked.

"Yes."

"Were you doing a fashion shoot or something?"

"No."

"She's very beautiful. Who is she?"

"Her name is Lian Jiang," he said.

Jack looked at the picture again, then at Gray. His whole body had changed. His mood was so defined by his shape that to Jack it was as if Gray had said, *I'm sad now*. He placed the binder on the bed, then downed the last of his *šlivo*. Gray got the bottle and poured him some more.

"I guess you miss her," Jack said.

"Yeah."

"I try to call my wife whenever the phones are up. Sometimes the sound of her voice is enough to break my heart."

"I haven't spoken to Lian in a long time. We went different directions."

"I'm sorry," Jack said. "Have you heard from that little French reporter you were hanging on to?"

"Suzzette? No."

"Look, let's get ripping drunk," Jack said. "Sit about and tell stories of women we've known."

"I'll get the other bottle."

Two days later Jack flew out of Sarajevo on a UN cargo plane. There had been a message from his wife that was vague and cryptic. Something about cancer. Looking through the small window at the night sky flying past, he was afraid he had made too many mistakes.

He landed in Zagreb and had to wait five hours to board the commercial flight to London. Being out of the war zone felt strange. He hadn't realized he'd been keeping his spine so stiff. When he relaxed into his seat on the plane, a cramp raced through his lower back. It left him sweating.

A flight attendant offered him a pillow, and he shook his head.

"Scotch, please," he said.

"Are you certain about the pillow?"

"Yes, just the scotch."

She brought him a small bottle and a cup with ice.

"Another bottle or two, please."

"I'm sorry?"

He held up two fingers, "Two more, please."

"It will cost extra."

"I don't mind."

It was late when he arrived home to a silent, dark house. He didn't turn on the lights, and he found himself in the living room uncertain where in the house the bedroom was and too tired to bother looking. He found the couch by bumping into it and stretched out there to sleep.

He moved slowly in the morning, rediscovered the rooms. The sudden snap of light switches and the appearance of light made him smile. Hot water from the taps was like finding lost gold, and he stripped off his foul clothes and showered until the water ran cool. When he pressed a towel to his wet face he was surprised the cloth didn't smell like death.

He carried all the clothes he'd brought home with him into the tiny laundry room off the kitchen and put them in the washing machine. He made himself breakfast: three fried eggs, toast, and half a package of sausage. As he ate, he wandered through the house until he finally settled in front of the television like a child. When he finished eating he went to stand in front of the closet in the bedroom and stared at the clothes hanging there. They were certainly his, but he could no longer imagine himself wearing them. Suits, slacks, polished shoes with slick soles. Those clothes weren't good for anything but sitting in a chair behind a desk. He'd never before felt so alienated from his peacetime self. He left the bedroom and went back to the laundry room, where he stood waiting for his clothes as if waiting to renew his driver's license.

Later Jack sat in a chair next to Veronica's hospital bed while she slept. He sat with his elbows on his knees, his hands folded. He was afraid it would be as bad as he imagined, and he wanted to wake her to see her eyes move over him.

Despite all of his time away over the years, he had learned the language of her face. She had always been a horrible liar. The tiny twitch between her eyebrows gave her away. Sarcasm tightened the corners of her mouth. Disappointment wrinkled her eyes. It was the rising degrees of her smile that he loved. The way sadness pulled her down broke his heart. The years and the fine wrinkles that had come to inhabit the corners of her face made her expressions more elaborate. If she were awake, he would know how serious things were.

"That's not a death vigil, I hope," she whispered.

He looked at her, the broken corner of a smile. "No," he said.

"I'm glad you made it home."

"Me too," he said. He stood up from the chair and leaned over to kiss her.

"I came in for my yearly," she said and reached out to touch his cheek with the back of her hand. "Sometime in the last year I grew a few cancer cells."

"Bad?"

"Well, there were some lumps on my uterus, some cysts and things. A lump in my right breast."

"The nurse said they already operated."

"Last night they took the lump out of my breast. Tomorrow the uterus."

Jack held her hand and rubbed his cheek against her soft skin.

"It wasn't that serious," she said.

"Perhaps not," he said and kept his eyes focused on the floor so she couldn't read his face.

Emil felt brittle as old glass in the cold morning air, and he set his feet down gently. The American journalist may have been impressed with Emil's drinking the night before, but he doubted either of them felt as impressed now.

The snipers hidden in the hills kept him close to buildings, always aware of where he stood in relation to them. He paused at an intersection where someone had scrawled PAZI SNAJPER on the wall with a piece of chalk. He sprinted across the open space. The impact of his feet on the pavement made the throbbing behind his eyes worse. When he got to the other side he leaned against the wall for a moment to let the pounding in his head subside.

At the Holiday Inn he went to the front desk and asked for Gray Banick. The clerk nodded and turned to go into a small room behind the desk. It seemed strange to Emil that, with the war going on, people would still do something like work in a hotel.

The clerk came back with a small envelope and handed it to him. The message inside let him know where the truck they used was parked, explained the wage Emil was to receive, asked if he'd like to join Gray for breakfast. Emil put the note in the pocket of his jacket and started for the stairs and the basement garage. Breakfast would have been nice, but he thought he'd better get a little more sleep and take the edge off his headache.

He found the Land Rover, climbed into the back, and lay on the seat, but he couldn't sleep. With his arm curled under his head he forced his eyes shut, felt the knot of muscle tighten in his neck. He thought of the way Mira used to hum in the mornings after she got out of bed. The way she tied her hair back with a piece of twine before kneeling to pull weeds from the garden. It surprised him to be thinking of her in the past tense. She was beautiful. She had strong hands.

Mira, he would say, touching her bare arm, *the knot is back.* She would press her strong fingers into the tight lump at the base of his neck and force the muscle to relax.

He dug his own fingers into the knot and tried to work it out. Eventually he gave up and climbed out of the truck. He sat on the hood trying to work the knot out by rotating his shoulders and swiveling his head.

As people began to come into the garage, he pushed himself off the hood and went to the door. Gray was one of the last. He didn't say anything about Emil not joining him for breakfast. He just nodded and walked quietly toward the truck and got in on the passenger side. Emil got in on the driver's side.

"Where shall we go?" Gray asked after Emil started the engine.

"Where are the others going?"

"They always seem to end up taking pictures of the same thing again and again. We should go other places."

Emil held the steering wheel and looked at him. "Where?"

Gray frowned and nodded. "Show me your Sarajevo. Show me the places reporters rarely go."

"If you wish."

"Please. Does your head hurt?"

"Yes."

Gray took a bottle of aspirin out of his jacket, held it out to Emil. "There's some water in my bag."

"I will be fine," Emil said. He took two tablets and swallowed them.

"Whenever you're ready; just take it easy for a while."

Emil put the truck in gear, drove slowly out of the garage and into the bright, cold day.

They crouched in an abandoned apartment. There was no glass in any of the windows, and the walls were uneven, shattered by bullets and shrapnel. The weather had swept into the room for months, and there was nothing left inside that wasn't water-damaged and warped. Snow had blown into the room and collected in the corners, turned to ice where the sun could not melt it.

Emil felt as if he were connected to an electrical wire. His skin itched under his clothes. The hair along his arms and the back of his neck seemed to crawl back into his skin and hide. The adrenaline in his body pushed back his headache and loosened the knot in his neck. He almost expected Gray to back out, to say he didn't want to get this close to the lines, but he said nothing. The American's face was indecipherable behind the dark sunglasses.

The clouds in the dull blue sky made gestures at snow. Through the window he could see the hills, gray as weathered bones.

They settled against the wall on either side of a window and carefully took glances outside. In the snow a few yards away were two dead soldiers. Their bodies frozen to the ground.

"We cannot stay here long," Emil whispered.

Gray nodded.

"Snipers will find us."

"Gotcha."

Gray held his camera a little way out the window, pressed down the button, and let the auto-winder pull the film through the clicking shutter. He finished a roll of film, and Emil watched him unload the camera.

"How much longer?" Gray asked.

"Until I get nervous."

Gray chuckled. "What about me?"

"You are nervous?"

"I think I shit myself about twenty minutes ago."

Emil frowned.

"I'm kidding. You seem very calm."

"I wanted to be an actor once."

He watched Gray load a new role of film, then snap a few more shots out the window.

"Ready?"

"You have taken all the pictures you want?"

"Yes, thank you."

They made their way out of the apartment and down to the basement of the building. They went through a hole that had been knocked through the foundation to allow access to the network of trenches marking the battle lines in this part of Sarajevo.

Emil led Gray away from the building, and they kept their bodies bent at the waist to stay below the edge of the trench. The sudden crack of automatic weapons made them crouch lower, but none of the rounds landed near them. There was return fire from the city. A few angry shouts. The thump of a mortar. Emil wanted to get away from the lines quickly. His facade of cool was reaching its ragged end, and he was afraid he would expose himself to the American as a coward.

They passed a few soldiers crouched around a dugout in the side of the trench, their eyes glassy and unconcerned with the presence of two strangers amid the sounds of fighting.

"Emil, stop."

He turned and crouched against the side of the trench and looked back to where Gray was kneeling to change the lens on his camera.

"American?" one of the soldiers asked.

"Yes," Gray said. "Do any of you speak English?"

"Little bits," the man said.

"Emil, I need you to translate, please."

Emil came back to Gray, kept his head below the edge of the trench.

A soldier with an ugly red scar down one cheek who seemed to be in charge of the six men there asked a question in Serbo-Croat. Emil answered the man.

"What did he say?"

"He wanted to know what you've been taking pictures of. I told him about the bodies in front of that building."

The soldier spoke to Emil again.

Emil translated for Gray, "He says those are their kills. There was an attack two days ago."

"Why do you leave them there?" Gray asked.

The leader spat on the ground and squinted one eye as he looked at Gray, then back down the trench line before he spoke.

"He said they shoot at them every time they come down for the bodies. They have a sniper near here in a very secret position."

Emil wondered if Gray was paying attention. As soon as he mentioned the sniper, Gray turned his head and looked down one arm of the trench and then the other. From where they were, slightly protected in the lee of a small building, Emil knew they did not have a good view of the other shattered buildings in the area. The new dugout still smelled of earth despite the cool temperatures.

"I know where your sniper is," Gray said.

"What?" Emil wiped sweat from his forehead.

"The only place that sniper could be to shoot those soldiers is the building we were in."

"So?"

"It isn't a secret. I'm sure the Serbs will try to take him out. They should move him soon."

Emil frowned but told the soldier. The man laughed, took out a pack of unfiltered cigarettes, and offered one to Emil, then Gray. They each took one.

"What's the joke?" Gray asked, and Emil translated.

"He says thank you for trying to help, but you underestimate our snipers," Emil said and spat a bit of tobacco off his tongue.

"United Nations?" the man asked, his English muddled by his accent.

"No," Gray said. "Newspaper. But I do have another question."

The man looked at Emil, and he translated. The man smiled, made a small gesture with his hand. An invitation.

"How easy is it to infiltrate through these lines?"

Emil asked the soldier. The man shrugged, looked away from them. The rifle fire that had been background noise to their conversation began to die off. Silence crowded into the trench. His voice dropped against the lack of noise, as if he were afraid of drawing fire.

"He says that if you really want to get out of the city on foot, it is best to use the tunnel at the airport, but if you are crazy enough to want to get in, you can just run."

Gray nodded, then smiled and held out his hand to the soldier. "Thank you," he said.

The soldier shook his hand.

Jack tried to sleep in an uncomfortable chair in the waiting room under the fluorescent lights. He wasn't thinking much about Veronica, even while he waited to hear that her second operation was finished. It was as if the war had pushed out a spot in his mind too big for anything else. Before, when he'd gone to Vietnam, then Cambodia, and a never-ending succession of small wars after that, he'd been able to drop everything and come home to her with no burdens. The horrible images still hung in his imagination, but it was almost as if they'd taken place in a movie. He had felt little in the way of remorse, indignation, or injustice. No self-righteous outrage. He'd been happy to go back to covering the slow politics of peace and spending his evenings at home.

Not with this war.

He stared at his shoes, the dried mud from Sarajevo still clinging to the edges, and tried to order the wars on the level of horror he'd witnessed. He realized this was the first war he'd covered in which the participants were nearly all white Europeans. Vietnam, Cambodia, Honduras, Chad, even the Falklands. He had gone into and come out of those wars, letting the brown otherness of one or both armies dampen his empathy. Now war had come home, settled itself in Europe for the first time since he was a child.

He wished he could have known his father better. What he knew of his father's war he had gotten from books and television documentaries. From Hollywood. His father had never spoken directly of the war. When he'd died, there had been only a footlocker packed with old uniforms and a few medals. There were photographs that echoed with the potential of memory locked in the familiar face of his father among other soldiers. Every photograph made him wonder what it was like to fight a war against someone who, stripped of his uniform, would never give himself away as different until he spoke.

He barely registered the presence of the doctor, the hand on his shoulder and the words he spoke. There was only the slow realization that he should go home.

A few days later Veronica came home, escorted by Nicole. Their daughter took up residence in her old room and helped around the house. Suddenly it was as if Jack wasn't needed. He would go into the kitchen, vaguely thinking he should make dinner, and Nicole would already be there, moving from the counter to the stove as if dancing. He would go to begin laundry, and Nicole would already be folding clothes.

"Can you afford to take this much time off work?" Jack asked her.

"I manage granddad's restaurant. I can take off whenever."

"When did this happen?"

"A year ago," she said.

"No one told me."

"I'm sure Mother mentioned it. You were probably off with some war."

He looked at his daughter and frowned. She had the same blond hair as her mother. The same eyes. The same stubborn disposition that sometimes made Jack want to stomp his foot like a two-year-old.

"I'm sorry," he said.

"It's okay. I'm used to it by now."

He walked over to the table and picked up a towel, folded it, laid it on the stack with the others. Nicole picked it up and refolded it.

"Do the socks," she said.

"What did I do wrong?"

"It wasn't square, Dad. They fit better in the closet that way."

He shook his head. "I'd better go check on your mother."

"I'm sure she's fine."

Jack stood for a moment, looked at his daughter, then turned to look down the hall to the stairs. Veronica was probably asleep, and it was rare that he saw Nicole anymore. He could remember her at seven, hair in a ponytail, wearing blue jeans and a t-shirt. A tomboy with dirt on her face. He wanted to tell her what he remembered best was that part of her. He wanted to make a joke of the idea that when a man has a daughter under ten, it is the only time a woman will love him without criticism.

He picked up a handful of socks and laid them on the table, "How then do I fold these?"

"Just make sure they match."

He listened to Veronica's breathing and watched the evolution of shadows in the corners of the room, diving into memories and the images they seemed to hold for him. Thoughts of returning to the war kept him awake. He had been in Sarajevo too long, had taken too many pictures of horrible things.

Jack thought of Gray, and that made him think about the photograph the younger man carried. Why did Gray's body seem to collapse when Jack asked about the woman? What had happened between them? Jack wanted to know if that picture had been the real reason the French reporter had left Gray so suddenly.

Veronica moved in her sleep. She turned toward him and rested her head against his shoulder, her arm across his chest. He had not realized how much he'd missed her. The feel of her breath across his skin and the way she fit against him, as if they had grown into the shape of each other, let him finally stop thinking.

But he couldn't sleep. He lay awake counting the beats of her heart.

"*You mean* you're not home for good?"

"No," Jack said.

"Why aren't you talking to Mom about this?"

Jack poured his cup of tea into the sink, then turned to face Nicole. "I suspect she knows without me telling her."

"Fucking hell, Dad. You always abandon her."

"I'm not abandoning her. I'm going back to work."

"In a war zone."

Nicole picked up the tray with Veronica's breakfast on it and started for the kitchen door but stopped. "Why don't you take breakfast to her today . . . and tell her you're going back to work."

Jack turned away from her and looked out the window at the small lot behind the house and at the house across the alley. He heard her push the door open and the sound of the china rattling as she walked away. There had been so many times in his life when he'd done things he'd immediately wished he could undo. So many of them had happened in this house, most of them with Nicole. It was easier to go away to a war than to learn how to talk to his daughter.

When he heard the door open again he turned, expecting to see Nicole there. Veronica leaned against the doorframe, Nicole behind her.

"Mom," she said, "you should go back to bed. I'm sorry."

"When are you leaving?" Veronica asked.

"Not right away."

"When, Jack? Tomorrow? The day after?"

"The third of January," he said.

"I really am sick of this, Jack. I had hoped that, at some point after you turned fifty, you would give up chasing wars. It was a little romantic when we were younger, but not anymore."

"What do you want me to do?"

"How many times have they offered you an editorship?"

"Twice."

"Tell them you'll take it."

"This war is important, Veronica."

"Fuck the bloody war. Have you ever understood how much I worry?"

"This will be the last one, I promise," he said.

"Your goddamn promises." She turned away from him and let the door swing shut. Nicole stopped it, stood in her mother's place, and glared at him.

"Happy fucking Christmas, Dad."

The air in the basement was dense with cigarette smoke. Emil could tell by the smell who smoked the locally made Drina cigarettes and who had managed to find the American-made Marlboros. Carefully he put his hand in the pocket where his own pack was and held them in his palm. He looked around for Gray, but the American had disappeared in the crowd and smoke.

There were so few familiar faces now. A few weeks ago Emil could have walked into a place like this and met a dozen people he knew. Now he guessed at faces in the dark and was wrong.

A large hand landed on his shoulder, and he turned. Goran was like an abstract artist's version of a crow. Gaunt, dressed in black. His long arms always crossed or held close to his body as if to conserve heat; his neck jutted his head forward from his shoulders and made him always look slightly hunched over.

"I thought you were dead."

"I am working for an American reporter," Emil said.

"Let me have a Marlboro then."

Emil took out his pack and gave a cigarette to Goran. As Emil held his lighter out, he noticed the woman. He offered her a cigarette, and she accepted.

"This is Katja," Goran said. "Her place was hit by artillery this morning."

"Do you have a place to stay?"

"Goran is helping me find a new place," she said.

He nodded, and the three of them stood for a moment and smoked, then Goran patted Emil's shoulder.

"There are some things I need to see about," he said. He turned to Katja. "Do you want to come along or stay here?"

"I will stay here," she said. "My feet are tired."

Goran stuck the cigarette in his mouth and walked into the darkness.

Emil stood next to Katja for a moment without saying anything. He smoked his cigarette, then dropped the butt on the floor and crushed it under his heel.

"Are you from Sarajevo?" he asked

"No. My family is from Bihać. I was attending university when the war started."

"I had just enrolled," he said. "Do you still have friends here?"

"Goran. A few people I work with at the Holiday Inn."

Emil squinted in the darkness, tried to make out the details of her face. He had to have seen her before, he was certain.

He woke a little before dawn, his mind still slippery from alcohol. Katja's head rested on his chest, her small hands were squeezed under his ribs to keep warm. He felt her breath, slow and steady. The weight of her body next to him was a sedative, and he pressed his nose into the scent of her hair. Cigarettes and wood smoke.

Stjepan stood in the doorway, his arms crossed. A pale shadow in the gray light that seemed to come from nowhere in particular. After a moment he turned and disappeared into the darkness. There were the sounds of the firebox being opened, a few handfuls of paper being wadded up. The sudden starburst of a match threw light out around his thin body.

Slowly Emil undid himself from Katja's arms, found his cold clothes on the floor, and dressed before going to sit with Stjepan.

"Who is she?" Stjepan asked.

"Her name is Katja."

The boy poured water from a plastic jug into a tin cup and placed the cup on the firebox to heat. Silently he stared at the shifting flame.

"For a moment I thought she was Mira."

Emil sat on the floor next to Stjepan. At the mention of her name Emil wanted to rip out his own heart and replace it with ice and immortality. He wanted to break out of Sarajevo and put the barrel of a rifle to the head of every Chetnik he could find. He wanted to condemn God himself for turning his back on the world.

"No, Stjepan."

The boy nodded. Emil reached out and placed his hand on the back of the boy's neck; he squeezed gently. "Be kind enough to make the coffee stretch for three. I will see what we have to eat."

"I will."

Veronica turned her back to him as she slept. The window behind them threw sunlight across the room. Jack watched the subtle movement of her body as she breathed. Her sharp shoulder blades edged out toward him like the residue of wings. She had given up being angry with him, she said, because she was too sick to care anymore, but Jack still kept a distance between them, not wanting to disturb her. He tried to sort his memories down to the one unsettling his sleep. It wasn't her distance. He'd suffered that before and knew there were ways to appease her. But something of her was bound up in it, something old, something that made him want to hold her and tell her about Gray.

I miscarried.

The words had entered him through the phone line from the other side of the world. An ominous message from home while he sat in a hotel room in Vietnam. The sound of explosions in the darkness.

Darling, this isn't the best time for me.

Nor is it the best time for me, Jack.

People are dying here.

I miscarried, Jack. I miscarried our son.

That's what it is, he thought. Gray had become a surrogate for that long-ago loss. His age would be close, maybe just a year or two off.

Their bodies in the dark mimicked shadows. Pressed against broken walls, they listened for footsteps in the new snow, for the suggestion of breathing. Above them, against the dark sky, were the crumbling silhouettes of old mosques side by side with the truncated spires of cathedrals.

"Not much farther," Emil said.

"I'm fine. Where are we going?"

"Gazi Husref Bey."

"Friend of yours?"

Emil smiled. "No. It is a mosque. Once we get there, we will be safe from snipers."

"Oh, sightseeing in the dark. Great."

"If you do not want to go, say so."

"Sorry."

Emil led Gray quickly across the street and into the shadows of another building. In the darkness Emil stepped carefully, tested his footing before moving forward through the crumbled building. Some of the buildings in old Sarajevo had basements, and the right amount of pressure on a seemingly solid pile of rubble could send a person down and the rubble down on top. He looked behind him to make sure Gray had followed.

He stopped where a doorway stood by itself and leaned against the old frame. A few yards away, the battered walls of the mosque seemed nearly whole in the darkness.

"Very lovely in the dark, Emil. Come on, let's not get shot here."

"I did not bring you here just to see it. We have something to do, and it is important."

"I'm sorry."

"I am not offended . . . yet."

Slowly he led Gray through the doorway, along a path through the rubble to the well. At the sudden scream of artillery overhead they crouched against the side of the well, watched the sky and the horizon of the city around them. The muffled sounds of explosions reached them, but they couldn't see the bright flashes of fire that marked impact.

Emil touched Gray's shoulder, leaned close to him, and spoke loudly against the sounds of gunfire. "This is a very special well. It is said that whoever drinks from the well here will always return to Sarajevo."

"I don't think I'll come back if I'm still going to be shot at."

"It will be the old Sarajevo again. I refuse to believe otherwise."

"I do hope so, Emil."

"And this is a way to make sure you will not forget us when you go back to America."

He knelt by the well, reached one of Gray's collapsible cups through the iron bars that encircled the top like a mushroom, and filled the cup. He gave it to Gray and watched him drink.

Gray and Emil sat in the restaurant of the Holiday Inn staring at the coffee mugs on the table. There was nothing but weak coffee for breakfast. The Bosnian Serbs had started their shooting early that day and seemed very enthusiastic, which meant the already thin supplies were not moving.

"What a sad-looking character you are," someone said.

Emil looked up at a tall white-haired man with a round belly and a camera bag over his shoulder.

"'Morning, Jack," Gray said. "When did you get back?"

"Last night, late. Before the shooting started. You were out."

"Jack, this is Emil Todorović. He's my assistant."

"Nice to meet you. Move over there, lad," Jack said and sat down next to Gray. He took a bottle of whiskey out of his camera bag, set it on the table. "Never leave home without it," he said.

"How was home, Jack?"

"Bloody awful. Let's not talk about it now." He poured whiskey into an empty coffee mug and looked around. "I guess if there's no more coffee, I'll have to make do. Anyone?"

"Sure." Gray slid his half-empty mug over, and Jack poured in a little whiskey.

"Emil? Or do you have religious objections?"

Emil slid his mug over to Jack. "I can't remember all of the rules."

"Good man," Jack said. "How long have you been working for Gray here?"

"About eight weeks."

Jack set down his mug. The way Jack looked at him, then around the room, puzzled Emil at first. The memory of how he'd come to this job was slow to surface.

"I suppose wars do happen without me."

"They do indeed, Jack," Gray said.

"Are you planning to leave Sarajevo anytime soon?"

"Hadn't really thought about it."

Emil cleared his throat. "You should go home."

"Wouldn't want to," Gray said.

"There's got to be someone back home who might like to see you after all this time," Jack said.

Gray looked at Jack, picked up his mug, and finished his coffee before he answered. "I think we'll take the day off; what do you think, Emil?"

"If you like."

Gray reached into his coat pocket, took out a little money, and handed it to Emil. "Paid day off."

"That is not necessary," Emil said.

"You've earned it."

Gray stood up, then walked across the lounge and was gone.

"He hasn't changed much," Jack said. "I guess I shouldn't have pressed him about going home."

"What is at home?" Emil asked.

"He hasn't told you?"

"No."

"A woman who broke his heart."

"Ah, the woman in the picture," Emil said.

They sat quietly for a moment, and Emil studied the old man. Around them were the sounds of war. The occasional shock-wave rattle of glass in a window. Sirens. Jack seemed uncomfortable, turning his head in the direction of the noises as if he might be able to see through walls, witness the danger.

"Thank you for the drink," Emil said. "I think I will go work on the Land Rover. It has not been running well."

The old man grunted, nodded his head. Emil got up and left him at the table.

"What happened to Dzevad?" Jack asked as he closed the door to Gray's room.

"He was shot the day after you left," Gray said.

Jack leaned against the wall and crossed his arms. "Were you with him?"

"We were coming back from the airport."

"Goddamn." Jack scratched his chin and looked around the room. He thought there should be more to say, that there should be more feeling in him, but all he felt was frustration.

He sat down on the bed nearest the door. "Gray, why do you stay here in Sarajevo?"

Gray took a deep breath, lifted a bottle of whiskey off the nightstand. He poured a shot into one of his collapsible cups and offered the bottle to Jack. The bottle was nearly full, and it felt cool in Jack's hand. He drank a bit and set it on the floor beside the bed.

"I don't know," Gray said. "It seems like something to do."

"Does that woman have anything to do with it?"

"Woman?"

"Don't be coy, son."

Gray picked up the bottle and poured a little more whiskey into his cup, then set the bottle back on the floor. After he drank, he sucked air through his teeth, pulled a bag over to his feet, and began to sort through it. The binder with the photos came out. Gray opened it and flipped quickly through the pages, then gave it to Jack.

"She didn't really have anything to do with me coming here, but if certain things hadn't happened, I'd still be in the States."

Jack looked at the binder in his hands but didn't open it. A strange gesture, he thought. It was almost as if Gray expected the binder and the photos inside to explain everything. It reminded Jack of himself.

"My wife is probably going to leave me because of this war."

Gray nodded as if he understood, then finished his drink.

"Maybe we should both go home," he said.

"Then we'd be miserable and bored."

"I'm sure there'd be something."

"Carnivals are exciting, I hear."

"And state fairs."

"Yes, I've heard of those. Cotton candy and things deep-fat-fried."

"The horror."

"Indeed."

Gray shook his head, started to smile, but it died quickly.

"Give me the bottle, please," he said.

Jack reached down, picked it up, and held it out.

Jack felt every bump in the path they drove along, every twitch of the suspension system. The clatter of automatic weapons crashed through his head. Bouncing across the uneven ground, all he could think about was the feeling in his stomach, like he'd swallowed steel wool. He sucked water from a squeeze bottle.

Emil drove the truck right into the crumbling shell of a building and stopped.

The crack of gunshots. Shouts. Explosions. Gray was out of the truck and Jack tried to catch up, pulling his camera bag after him as he pushed open the door. His feet caught on the frame, and his weight threw him out of the truck. He landed on his shoulder and turned, pulled the camera bag onto his stomach. Gray came around the truck and helped him up, then they crouch-walked to where Emil knelt behind the remnant of a wall.

They huddled behind the wall and carefully peeked over the top.

They were almost two hundred yards from a few houses that butted up against a grove of trees. In this part of Sarajevo, the front lines reached almost into the hills. There was no breeze along the ground, but the bare trees moved as if touched by wind. Smoke, pale gray, spilled into the sky from a few of the buildings.

"What are we looking at here?" Jack asked.

"Serbs are trying to break in," Emil said.

"Just sounds like object lessons to me."

"I get some army gossip," Emil said and pointed toward the houses. "That house was made into a bunker."

"Scuttlebutt," Jack said. "I need my water."

Gray put his hand on Jack's shoulder. "Wait."

The shooting ebbed, almost seemed to stop completely, and then suddenly there was the hollow, echoing thump of a mortar round landing among the buildings. Then another. The soldiers came out of the trees, nearly silent, as if they expected no resistance.

Jack held his camera on them, the action made large and grainy through his telephoto lens. He burned a roll of film and dropped the camera on the ground at his feet. His second camera hung from his neck, and he brought it to his eye. The lens was less powerful, and he quickly switched it out with another zoom lens from his bag.

They could see a group of fighters rushing into positions around a single building. They crouched against the walls, staying away from the windows and doorways as one man, apparently in charge, pointed and yelled.

Jack burned the roll of film in his second camera and swore to himself as he dropped below the wall to reload.

"Here." Emil held out Jack's reloaded first camera.

Jack took the camera and stood up. The assault started. Men lunged up from the ground, underhanded grenades through doorways and windows, then dropped back out of sight. Explosions, then smoke and flames shot out of the windows and doors. A few men rushed into the building so fast it seemed as if they would move into the last flying pieces of their own grenades.

Jack burned another roll and looked down to see Emil holding the other camera out to him.

The assault seemed to have stalled. The shooting from inside the building was furious, then it vanished. Swallowed completely into nothing. A single fighter stumbled out of the building, blood on his face and hands, and collapsed down the steps to land on the grass. For a long moment they existed in a pocket of silence, though fighting went on around them. The hollow mortar thump, the sharp clap as grenades landed, the stuttering talk of the assault rifles almost in the background and forgotten inside the sudden void brought by the bloody, stumbling fighter.

Jack almost took his finger off the shutter button, but then there was a single shot, then another, and then a wall of noise. The silence collapsed and filled with crashings and screams. The remaining fighters against the building crumpled, tried to run away. The fighters who covered them from other buildings stood still, confused. They tried to locate the source of the counterattack and walked into their own deaths.

Jack passed down his camera; the backup slapped into his hand.

The fighters fell back, drew themselves into the tree line as if they were a carpet rolling up. Their dead and the wounded who couldn't walk were left sprawled amid the buildings. Then everything was heavy silence.

Jack took his finger off the shutter button. "God damn it all to hell," he said.

He eased himself down and sat with his back against the wall. Emil handed his camera back to him, loaded, then handed two cameras back to Gray. There were two clusters of film canisters in front of Emil. He picked up six canisters and gave them to Jack, then gave the rest to Gray.

"A truly beautiful job," Jack said. "Thank you."

"You owe me four rolls of film," Gray said.

"What?"

Gray grinned and reached over to shake Jack's camera bag. The compartment where Jack kept his film was still zipped shut. "Leave it with Emil next time."

"Jesus Christ, you're making me feel like a rookie," Jack said.

"You're just a little rusty," Gray said.

"Or senile," Emil said.

"Bugger off, the both of you."

It was late when they came out of the makeshift darkroom the press corps had set up and climbed the stairs to Jack's room to have a drink. With loupes, they scanned their contact sheets for good shots.

"Have you thought about getting out of Sarajevo?"

Gray shrugged, sat back against the wall, and picked up his drink. "Yeah, a little."

"It'll certainly get you some rest. I think sometimes Sarajevo is a kind of poster child for the war. Bad enough to earn sympathy, but not so bad as to cause the kind of disgust one might get from Srebrenica, or Zenica, or especially Mostar."

"True."

Jack slipped his loupe into a pocket and stacked his contact sheets. He watched Gray. Gray's hair had not been cut in a long while and was starting to brush the collar of his shirt where it curled out from under the purple, sweat-stained cap he liked to wear. With the constant dark smears under his eyes, Gray never really looked alive. But he was there smoking a cigarette, his elbows across his knees. Gray never once seemed to need anything, yet Jack felt an incredible urge to protect him. To console him. To be fatherly.

When Gray had first arrived in Sarajevo, Jack had thought he would turn out to be some blustering American. He'd been wrong. Right away Gray had gone to the most horrible scenes and walked away from them as if he'd just been to a movie. He hardly talked to anyone at first except to answer a few questions about where he was from and who he was working for.

Then the French reporter, Suzzette, had pulled Gray out of his isolation. Jack had met her a few times earlier in the war. A tall woman, aggressive as a man. Jack wasn't even sure Gray was the same person when he came across them together. She would share his cigarettes, take them right from between his fingers. She would share his drinks the same way. For the month she and Gray were an item, it was nearly impossible to tell if they ever left each other's presence. The look on her arrowed features pulled down to sadness as she touched Gray's cheek with the back of her hand as if she were caressing a sleeping child.

Medicine, Jack thought. She was a kind of medicine that left him before he had a chance to heal. Gray never acted as though he missed her.

"It's time I get to bed." Gray crushed out his cigarette and collected his contact sheets. "I'll see you tomorrow, Jack."

"Unless we get blown up in our sleep."

Jack watched him leave, then got up and left his room. He did feel tired, but he didn't feel like being alone. Downstairs, at a table in a dark corner of the deserted lounge, he found a few reporters he knew from previous wars. Most of them had gotten fat, like he had. He showed them his contact sheets and watched them shake their heads. He knew they would tell him he was getting too old to be running around so close to the lines. When they finally did, he smiled and told them they had lost their nerve.

But it was a chore, trying to keep up with Gray and Emil. Jack was interested in the bond between them. A mutual empathy. On some mornings he would get out of his room late and find the two of them in the lounge talking, or already in the garage at the truck, checking the engine. He wanted to step out a little farther from this safety.

In Vietnam he'd gone into the jungle with the troops, lived with them there. Seen the confusing flash of sudden combat and carried a rifle over his back because it felt safer than just his camera. And once, at night, he'd fired the rifle at a shadow when his own fear had seized him by the kidneys. He wanted to feel that again, wanted to deny the age that had crept up on him.

Day after day Emil took Gray and Jack to the sounds of explosions, to the places where snipers had attacked. He began to understand the special cynicism of these journalists and how similar it was to that of the residents of Sarajevo. The futility they saw in everything that was done. The necessity to do it anyway. The Western countries would have ignored the war if they could, but these journalists kept sending back pictures and words. Even though there seemed to be very little effect, they kept doing it: naming Milošević, Karadžić, and Mladić as murderers, naming the atrocities again and again no matter how many times the politicians said there was no way to make sense of this war among neighbors. He understood them even more as his own depression and cynicism made him aware that the stress of survival had dissolved into an almost passive acceptance of death.

At the end of every day, exhausted down to the center of his bones, Emil would go home along familiar streets, barely paying attention to the scrawled messages warning of snipers. At home he'd find Stjepan, his eyes unfocused and staring into the small fire burning in the tiny makeshift stove in the middle of the living room. Emil would collapse on the pallet he'd set up for himself and Katja and be asleep before the small fire burned out. He would wake up in the morning to find Katja had materialized next to him.

Stjepan barely spoke then. After coming to Emil and telling the story of their village, he spoke only when he needed information. He barely ate. In the mornings before Emil left, Katja would catalog the things Stjepan had said or eaten the day before. And then, if he could, Emil would bring food, a few fresh eggs Gray had gotten, a few withered vegetables. The money secreted away for later, for an emergency.

Some nights Emil would wake to the sound of fighting. A bullet hitting one of the boards he'd nailed over the windows. Then, unable to sleep, he would stare into the dark shadows that hid in the corners, their shapes mutating, and remember certain nights with Mira. They would find a tree to sit under and look through the canopy of leaves at the stars and the moon. They would talk about the future as if it were inevitable, as if it were an expected child they never thought would be miscarried.

In the mornings Emil would get out of bed and start a small fire and watch Stjepan and Katja sleep. Other times the boy would wake with him, and they would sit and stare into the flames.

"I want to join the army," Stjepan said one morning, his voice brittle from disuse.

"You are too young."

"I saw a boy with a rifle the other day. He was about my age."

"Where?"

"I went to get water."

"Stjepan, I told you not to leave the apartment unless you were with me or Katja."

"You are never here."

"You cannot join the army."

"You cannot stop me."

"Then I will beg you if I have to. Wait a year. Maybe the war will be over then."

"Maybe the war will never end," Stjepan said. He turned away from Emil and crawled back to his bed.

Jack watched the single candle burn down almost to nothing and waited for it to die completely. The artillery that shelled parts of the city no longer bothered him. He had been able to sleep through worse shelling before. There was something else keeping him awake, and he kept trying to push through the half-remembered conversations, the comments he wished he had made that day, to pinpoint the one thing gnawing at him.

Gray. Something he'd said. Everything in his imagination swirled around one moment in his mind that he couldn't catch. He sat up on the edge of the bed and felt around for his flashlight, found it, turned it on. The contact sheets and the few prints he'd made that day were across the room on the table, and he stumbled over, his legs stiff and sore from so much walking and standing.

One of the photographs would help, he was sure. It seemed as if all of his memories were kept that way. His life burned onto film, filed in boxes. The people who looked at his photographs in the newspapers back home could never be connected to them the way he was. Each one, for him, carried the story of himself in the past. His photograph of a Cambodian man squatting next to a row of skulls on the ground was a kind of family portrait. The man had been Jack's guide, the skulls, so the man claimed, his brothers who had been killed by the Khmer Rouge. For Jack, the image always extended to the moment he never had a photograph for: cradling that man's body in the jungle, feeling the life spasm out of him and leak into the ground as he whispered his brothers' names, as if greeting them in the dark.

Jack found the photograph he was looking for. It was in black-and-white, but his imagination filled in the colors.

They had found a place to relax in the sun the previous afternoon when the temperature had dared to climb out of the low 40s, a walled courtyard with a small plum tree in one corner. The walls and the buildings around it hid them from the snipers in the hills, and they had set down their camera bags and tried to forget the war.

Emil tended to a plum tree in the yard. He scraped at the bark with a knife, then dug below the layer of snow and sifted the soil underneath with his hands and held it to his nose.

What do you suppose he's doing?

I think his family were farmers, Gray said.

What did your family do?

There wasn't any real family trade. Yours?

Soldiers, until I came along.

My father was a cop. He was killed seven years ago on a drug raid.

Were you close to him?

No. Hell, I'm closer to you than I was to my father.

Jack then lifted his camera and took a picture of Gray.

Jack held the photograph in his dark hotel room, the beam from his flashlight catching the smooth surface as he moved, blanking it out. That had been what was keeping him up. The fatherless son. The sonless father. He wanted to reach out to Gray, put his arm around the younger man's shoulder, and . . . do what? That was the thing Jack couldn't figure out. What did he have to teach Gray? What could he pass on to him that would be of any significance? *Maybe,* Jack thought, *that is the reason to try.* To find out what he really knew of the world.

The morning sunlight was in their eyes as Emil steered the truck out of the garage, and almost immediately there was the sound of an explosion. They watched the sky for smoke and finally spotted the dark cloud as it rose from the part of town where Emil lived. He didn't wait for them to decide if they wanted to go see what had happened. Stjepan could have been nearby, or Katja, and he had to make sure they were alive. As he drove closer, speeding down alleys and through intersections, he became more worried. It was so close to home. So close to the market Katja frequented to buy food.

He stopped the truck at the end of an alley that emptied into the square where the market was. It was pointless to drive any closer. The square was crowded with people, and the truck would only get in the way.

The survivors were already carrying off the wounded as he got out of the truck and pushed his way through the fringes of the crowd. His feet slipped, and when he regained his balance he looked down to see the ugly red smears on the street. He stopped, suddenly lost.

The sounds finally crashed through. Screaming. The slap of tennis shoes on the asphalt. The soft pleading of people in shock. He stood and scanned the swarm of people around him, trying to find Stjepan or Katja among the wounded and dead.

He saw Gray and Jack enter the crowd, almost impersonally, cameras raised to hide their faces as they stopped to photograph a woman with her right leg missing below the knee, a young man, maybe her son, dragging her away. It was familiar and strange at the same time, like déjà vu in a dream resembling a memory. The echo of an echo.

"Emil." Gray's voice pierced him, and he looked to see Gray stuffing his camera into his camera bag. "Here."

There was a child at Gray's feet. A girl. The look on her face swirled under blood. Confused. The girl held her own mangled arm against her chest. She sat next to a woman whose blood still oozed in tiny rivers from under her body.

Emil moved. His feet slipped under him, but he kept his balance. As he came closer he saw the infant on the other side of the dead woman, eyes shut, covered in blood.

"Take her," Gray said and stepped over the woman to pick up the baby.

"Is the baby alive?"

"Yeah, I think so. Take the girl to the truck."

Emil picked up the girl, and a scream broke loose from her throat. He carried her back through the bloody market to where they'd left the truck, wondering stupidly how he would open the door with the screaming girl in his arms. Then, suddenly, Jack ran past him, reached the truck first, and swung the door open for him to slip the girl onto the backseat. When everyone was in, Emil cranked the engine and shoved the transmission into reverse. He shot backward down the alley to the next intersection and spun the wheel to turn onto the street.

He did not worry about the roads he took. His ears were filled with the screams of the wounded girl in the backseat, her small body sheltered under Jack. Gray held the baby in his arms, and at last she began to cry. Emil sped wildly down exposed streets, swerved around debris.

The faint sound of rifle fire followed them. He cut corners, bounced the truck over curbs, ignored the whine and smell of burning rubber coming from the engine. Finally he ran the truck onto the sidewalk in front of the building that had become, in desperation, a hospital. They carried the children inside.

Then, suddenly, everything was calm. The children had been taken from them by doctors and nurses, leaving the three men alone in the entryway, abandoned. Gray put his hand on Emil's shoulder and squeezed. It felt like permission to breathe again.

They walked outside and sat on the curb by the truck. A pack of cigarettes was held out to Emil, and he took one, noticed the blood dried on his hands, the smell. He put the cigarette in his mouth and lit the end from the Zippo Jack held out to him.

"I think we set a record," Gray said.

"Have some new holes in the Rover," Jack said.

Emil looked up from the street and saw a new silver-ringed hole in the back of the truck and realized he still didn't know about Stjepan or Katja.

"We need to go back," Emil said.

"Yes," Gray said.

They got in the truck, and Emil drove them slowly back to his neighborhood, his mind numb. Prepared for the worst.

Gray gave him a pack of cigarettes as they stood in the lobby of the Holiday Inn.

"We're not going out today."

"Am I being fired?"

"No, no. There are some things Jack and I need to take care of, and we have to wait on the satellite phone."

"Are you leaving?"

"Yeah, it looks that way." Gray put his hand on Emil's shoulder. "Come on, let's see if we can get some coffee since you came all the way out here."

"I would not be angry if you left," Emil said.

"It makes me feel like shit to be able to leave here while you can't."

"It is my country's war. Not yours. Perhaps the war will end now, perhaps the Americans will finally get involved."

"Maybe. Listen, if you feel like it, stop by tomorrow. I may still need your help in the next couple of days."

"Yes."

"Have you been to the hospital to see the children?"

"No, not yet. I will go."

"I hope they have some family still alive."

"I do as well."

"I'm sorry it took so long to find out Stjepan and Katja were okay," Gray said.

Emil shrugged. "That is war."

They walked into the restaurant and sat down at a table.

Emil made the trip to meet Gray in the lobby on a few mornings over the following week, and Gray always had something for him, things that kept Emil, or Stjepan, or Katja from having to stand in a queue that day. Katja also was able, from time to time, to bring things home from her job at the Holiday Inn. It made life easier.

On a quiet night at the end of the week, the three of them sat in Emil's dark apartment, only the faint glow from a few homemade candles casting small shadows across their bodies. Stjepan sat with his knees drawn up, staring at the candle flame.

He had become more sullen since the conversation with Emil about joining the army. Emil understood. The army would be an outlet for revenge, so that Stjepan could extract the knife from his heart. Though the wound would never heal, he could ease the sharpness of the pain. It was also an opportunity for him to do something other than sit and worry. The worry would still be there, but activity would allow the mind to forget.

"I would like to go dancing again," Katja said.

"We could try to get into the BB. Curfew is still an hour away."

"But then we would have to be there until the morning. I do not want to be there till morning."

"We could find someplace to sleep."

"It is not that. I want to be able to come home, like before the war. To go out and come home in the same night. Sleep in a bed that does not have lice, or fleas. I want to be normal again."

"I know."

Emil lit a cigarette and placed the pack on the floor by his feet. Stjepan reached across and picked it up, took out a cigarette and gave it to Katja, then took one for himself.

"Stjepan?"

"I am smoking," he said. "There is nothing else to do. The snipers could kill me tomorrow. Cancer will not."

"And joining the army might get you better food."

"Yes."

"When Gray and Jack leave, I will probably join. That way I can watch out for you, but I have one request."

"Yes?"

"Wait until after your fourteenth birthday."

"That is nine months away."

"Yes."

"The war could be over by then."

"Yes, but as much as you want to join, I do not."

Stjepan looked away from the candle, and Emil tried to look through the darkness to see his cousin's eyes. He knew he would not be able to keep the boy from joining forever.

Gray came to Emil's apartment at the end of the week, and they sat around the firebox in the dark and talked. Mostly it was nonsense. The last thing they wanted to talk about was the war. On that night Gray stayed late, and they made a place for him to sleep next to the firebox.

"Are you leaving Sarajevo soon?" Emil asked.

"Yes."

"Things will be tough while you are gone."

"The new cease-fire looks promising, though," Gray said.

Emil stared at Gray for a moment, smoked his cigarette. "Mladić and Karadžić will not honor it for long, and we are still under siege."

"Yes, I know. Unfortunately, my newspaper doesn't share that view."

"What will you do?" Emil asked.

"I am waiting to see if they will allow me to go to central Bosnia or if they will just tell me to come home."

Emil shrugged. "And if they tell you to come home, what will you do?"

"I may take a vacation instead. Go to Amsterdam."

Emil sat on a cushion next to the firebox and looked at the water starting to boil in the small tin pot.

"I would like to see Amsterdam someday."

"I wish I could take you all with me."

"We wish that you could as well."

Gray nodded.

Emil looked across the dim glow of the firebox at Katja. "Let us not talk about it now. We should enjoy these last hours together."

They sat in the dark apartment and talked late into the night.

After Jack and Gray left Sarajevo, Emil busied himself with trying to locate any family of the two children they had rushed to the hospital after the market attack, but things were not promising. The oldest child's arm had to be amputated. Her name was Sanela Dudić, and she said the baby was her sister, Anja. Emil took a few pictures of the children, and of their dead mother that Gray had left him, and returned to the neighborhood where the market had been. The most anyone could tell him was the woman had begun coming to the market a few days before the attack.

He went to the Parrot Building, in the old part of town, where a number of refugees had taken up residence, and asked around, but no one knew anything. He gave their names and pictures to the UN at the airport. After almost a month no one had turned up, and the children were placed in an orphanage.

By the end of March the fighting had started again. The Bosnian Serbs moved on Goražde, took UN and NATO hostages in some areas around Sarajevo. Emil wondered if Gray and Jack would come back, and so he began showing up at the Holiday Inn once or twice a week to ask some of the other reporters if they had been in contact with his departed friends. There was some news from Jack, a couple of letters and packages some of the reporters were able to get into the city. Emil was sure Jack had sent more, but some of the packages must have been confiscated at various checkpoints in and around the city. It was a toll extracted by the militias and gangs that had become the de facto security for some neighborhoods in the absence of legitimate Bosnian Army troops.

There was no direct word from Gray. A letter from Jack bore the news that Gray had, indeed, gone to Amsterdam for a few weeks, but afterward even Jack had lost touch with him.

Emil never received the letter Jack sent saying he would return in late May, so he was surprised when Katja came home with the news that Jack was, once again, staying at the Holiday Inn. Emil hurried to see him.

Jack was in the restaurant when Emil arrived, right where Emil thought he would be.

"Any word from Gray?" Emil asked.

"He was in Paris," Jack said. "I guess you didn't get my letter?"

Emil shook his head.

"Well, let me get you caught up then," Jack said. He took a couple of packs of Marlboros out of his shirt pocket and gave them to Emil.

"Thank you."

"There's more." Jack took a wad of money out of another pocket. "Gray says it's back pay."

"I do not understand. Is Gray not coming?"

"Not to Sarajevo." Jack lit a cigarette and gave Emil the lighter. "Gray is on his way to Tuzla. We're supposed to meet him there."

Emil stared at Jack for a moment, uncertain of many things. "How?"

"Well, I've been trying to find a way to do that with as little danger to you as possible. No one is cooperating."

"I could get out through the tunnel, if I had money."

"Don't the Serbs keep the exit pretty well hammered with artillery?"

"What do they not keep well hammered with artillery, Jack?"

"Okay. What other options are there?"

"I could swim across the river."

"That sounds worse than the tunnel. Listen, you know you don't have to do this. He knows you've got Katja and Stjepan to look after."

"I will think about it, and I will need to talk to them."

"When can you let me know?"

"Tomorrow."

"I'll see about getting you a pass for the tunnel then. It's better than swimming."

"I cannot believe you are going to do this," Katja said.

"I will leave the money for you and Stjepan."

"It is not that, Emil. Is there not enough war for you right here?"

"There are things I cannot find the answers to here."

"And what will you do if she is alive?"

"I am not sure," he said and touched Katja's cheek. "What would you do if Petar were to arrive here?"

"I do not know."

"You will be fine here," Emil said.

"What about you?"

"I will not die in this war. I promise."

"How are you leaving?"

"The tunnel. Jack will be waiting for me on the other side."

In the dim light from the candles it was easy to see she was crying. Her tears sparkled, golden. He took her hand and pulled her close, held her.

Excavations

The morning is cool with a thin fog against the ground. Emil leaves the small boardinghouse where they spent their first night in Potočari and walks slowly down the street toward the bakery where Goran wants him to deliver the package. He wants to see whom he is to do business with and whether anything resembling authority might be watching the area.

Two years before these streets stank as thousands of desperate people crammed into the town. With no running water and very little food, the Bosnian Serbs squeezed the Muslims in day by day; the refugees could do little to move from the small spots they'd claimed on the streets. People ate, slept, relieved themselves where they were. They watched the hills for Mladić and his army and pleaded with the UN garrison for help when the Serbs came to deport them. The Dutch troopers did little but write down the names of some of the men the Serbs took off in buses.

There is a feeling like a stone under the skin of his belly, nausea as the memories surface and he tries to push them back down.

There were days like this one, cool with fog and tension stretched tight as violin strings, other days of constant sunlight and loose heat. Emil felt panic the moment he and Gray arrived inside the Srebrenica enclave.

You're not losing your nerve on me, are you?

Nerve? No. I am only saying I have a bad feeling.

Don't start being superstitious, Emil.

It is not superstition, Gray. It is . . . intuition.

Emil arrives at the bakery, pushes open the door, and stands for a moment on the tiled floor looking at the walls and the small counter. The air inside is warm and sweet from the baking. A young girl is placing loaves of bread in a basket. She smiles at him.

"How much are those?" he asks.

"Ten," she says.

"I would like three, please."

She takes a paper bag from below the counter and begins putting the loaves into it. As Emil takes out his money, a man moves through the doorway behind the counter. He stands there behind the girl with his arms folded across his chest, wrinkling the white apron. Emil wants to ask the man when he wants his package, but he won't do it in front of the girl.

"Dobro jutro," the man says.

"Dobro jutro."

"It looks to be a beautiful day."

"Yes," Emil says, holding out some money to the girl.

"Have you been to Potočari before?"

Emil still holds out the money. The girl behind the counter holds the bag. He watches her eyes as she looks from him to the man. The man must not come to the counter and speak to customers often, Emil thinks. He takes the money back and adds another bill.

"During the war," he says.

The girl reaches for the money and holds out the bag to Emil.

"Hvala," Emil says and steps back from the counter, then turns and puts his hand on the door.

"What unit were you with?" the man asks.

Emil looks out the door so the man won't see his face. "I wasn't with any unit," he says.

"Are you one of those people coming back to look for the dead?"

Emil grips the door handle, glances over his shoulder at the young girl behind the counter. "No," he says.

Emil walked out of Hiba Bašić's house and across the yard to where Gray sat in an old kitchen chair. His legs were stretched out in front of him and hooked at the ankles, arms crossed over his chest.

Have you been out here all night? Emil asked.

Think so. Couldn't sleep, Gray said.

You will catch cold this time of year if you are not careful.

Probably so.

Emil looked in the direction Gray was facing and saw the hills standing up in the golden morning light.

Have you been taking pictures?

No, but it's a beautiful sunrise.

Yes.

Pull up a seat, Emil. Watch it with me.

I only came out to tell you that Jack and I have returned and that we've brought some supplies.

Did you get my letter out all right?

Yes.

Gray nodded; then, as if by magic, a bottle appeared in his hand and he brought it to his lips. It must have been on the ground where Emil couldn't see it. Gray took a drink and then held the bottle out to Emil. It was nearly empty, so Emil finished it off and dropped it on the ground.

I don't think I'll ever understand people, Gray said. *We all want the same things in the end, but somehow we don't see that basic fact in each other. Especially if we convince ourselves to be afraid of the surface differences, like religion or race.*

You are drunk, Emil said.

Yes, a little, I suppose, but it doesn't change anything.

No, it does not.

Emil put his hands in the pockets of his coat and kicked at the ground. There was nothing more to say. He could only stand quietly by his friend and listen even though it felt like the hardest thing to do.

I need to quit feeling sorry for myself, Emil. It's pitiful.

Sometimes there is nothing else to do, Emil said. *Come, there's food inside. Hiba is making us breakfast.*

Slowly Gray stood up. His balance was shaky, and he shuffled to one side before Emil reached out and took hold of his arm. They walked back to the house like an old married couple. Inside, Hiba was stoking the fire in an old iron oven, and Jack was unpacking the boxes of supplies. They stopped what they were doing and looked at Emil as he helped Gray through the doorway. Emil watched the expressions on their faces melt from curiosity to concern.

I will make coffee first, Hiba said.

You're not going to be sick, are you, son? Jack asked.

I'll be fine, Gray said. *I just need to get cleaned up.*

He took his arm out of Emil's grip and slowly went through the room and into the next. Emil listened to him climb the stairs to the second floor.

I tried to get him to come in, Hiba said, *and he kept telling me he would come in a moment. I finally fell asleep waiting.*

He is stubborn, Emil said.

That's one way to put it, Jack said.

All this because of a woman? Hiba asked.

Emil shrugged. *I am sure there is more.*

Jack shook his head and began to break down the cardboard boxes for kindling. *If he's not careful, he's going to get himself killed.*

Sunlight fractures through the trees, drops misshapen motes on the ground where they walk. There is a silence hanging over everything like a damp curtain. Emil leads them into the forest and tries to remember the landmarks. Lian follows him, and Jack trails them both. Even now, two years later, there are bones on the ground in this part of the forest. The UN workers are making slow progress across the killing fields, cataloging the bodies while families hope for some lucky identification.

"They say this place is haunted." Emil stops where the ground drops away and he can see off in the distance a small, squat building on top of another hill. "It is good you did not make it here with us, Jack."

"How is that?"

Emil shrugs, takes out a cigarette and lights it. "It was desperate here."

Jack taps his cane against a tree. "It was desperate everywhere."

"Not like here."

"I don't want to be in these woods when it gets dark," Lian says.

"No," Emil says. "We will go back before dark. It is best to look in the daylight anyway."

Emil leads them through the trees, slowly now so Jack can keep up. He is silent and walks with his hands in his pockets. Lian walks with Jack, and Emil listens to him tell her about Bosnia.

"These three countries have been pushing against each other since the twelfth century. Orthodox Christian Serbs versus the Roman Catholic Croats and both of them against the Bosniaks, who are not all Muslim even though the TV shits back home tell it that way. Emil's people, well, they're old heretics of a sort. There used to be a Bosnian Church, but it all fell apart when the Bogomils showed up. They were a kind of mystic sect of Christianity that denied the crucifixion ever happened. Of course all of that gets confused and debated between the Serbs, Macedonians, Croats, and Bosniaks. What remains, when you get right down to the meat, is that the Roman Catholics and the Orthodox Christians both saw the Bosniak followers of the Bogomil sect as a threat and set about destroying them. Almost succeeded too, except the Turks invaded. The Turks and the Bosniaks got along so splendidly that a number of Bosniaks converted to Islam, which gave them a favored status in the Ottoman Empire. They were made governors of some of the other Slavic regions the Turks had conquered. Rewarded with land and titles. They were even charged with collecting a special tax the Ottomans leveled against the Christians for being Christian. After the Ottoman Empire pulled back from these parts, it was just a matter of time before things got bad for the Bosniaks.

"Before and after World War I and, of course, during World War II, whole villages were slaughtered by one group or another. The ethnic Serbs, called Chetniks, killed the Muslims, and the Muslims killed the Chetniks. The Chetniks and Croats killed each other. It wasn't until Marshall Tito, Croatian by the way, took control after the war that there seemed to be any kind of harmony."

Emil stops at the edge of a clearing and waits. Beyond him the open field is crowded with trucks and men digging. Their shovels throwing dirt at the sky. Others are on their hands and knees, sifting through the disturbed earth, sorting the bones of the dead.

"This is the place, I think," Emil says. "This is the last place we were together."

It's hard *to believe there could be any humanity left here,* Jack whispered to Gray.

Like watching the end of the world, Gray said. *I heard about something like that happening out west. Don't remember where.*

They huddled together, separate from Emil and the Bosnian soldiers, deeper in the house so the small light they shared could not be seen by the Serbs and draw fire. They smoked cigarettes and sipped from a flask of whiskey. Jack knew it would take a long time to forget what he had seen earlier that evening. A young man, who'd been held captive by the Serbs, had been sent walking across the no-man's-land between the armies. It had looked promising until they could hear him calling to his friends and see the condition of his body. His face swollen from bruises, his arms bent in ways that could happen only if they were broken, and a bomb strapped to his chest. There was nothing anyone could do but wait for the bomb to go off.

I think I'm getting too old for this, Jack said. *Maybe I'll skip out on the trip to Srebrenica.*

Gray sat quietly. Jack couldn't tell if he was being ignored or if Gray just had no response.

Don't you think it's a little risky?

No more than anything else around here, Gray said.

Jack took the flask from the floor and unscrewed the cap. *I think I'm finally getting tired of this war.*

It is a dismal little place.

Don't you think it's time to get out? Go home.

Gray looked up, shrugged. *Emil has been here for the whole thing.*

But it's his country, his war. You should go home.

No point, Jack. I've told you that before.

Heartbreak isn't a permanent condition.

Gray stretched out on the floor with his jacket rolled under his head. *War's not a permanent condition either.*

You're so bloody cryptic.

They are quiet in the room Jack and Emil share in the small boardinghouse. Emil and Lian sit on the floor, Jack on the bed because of his legs. The curtains are pulled shut against the darkness of the night.

Lian rubs her feet, pushes her thumbs hard against her arches, and sucks air through her teeth. "That was so awful today."

"Yes," Jack says.

Earlier she watched him slip the prescription bottle out of his bag, take a pill, then drink from his flask. She didn't say anything, and now she watches his eyes slide nearly shut.

"And this country has a long memory for perceived injustices," Jack mumbles.

Jack and Gray sat in the truck while Emil went up the path to his house with a few other Bosnian fighters. How long ago had the Serbs cleansed the village? Jack wondered. A year?

It was a two-story house, built of stone and wood. A little more than a century old, Emil had told him, and his family had kept it even during World War II, when the Nazis and their Ustashe militia tried to take everything, and later when the Chetniks tried to kill everyone, and finally when Tito had liberated them.

Jack listened to the wind in the trees, the sound of trucks in the distance. Gunfire far off in the hills. Everything distant, butting against their pocket of silence.

We might lose ourselves an interpreter, Jack said.

What do you mean?

He's going to want to get back at the Serbs.

He's wanted that for a while, Jack.

He'll want more.

Everyone always wants more.

They watched Emil come out of the house. He stood for a moment just outside the door, let his rifle slip from his hands and clatter down the steps to the ground. Slowly he raised his hand and waved Jack and Gray to him.

As they moved up the gravel path to the house, the other Bosnian soldiers came out of the front door and down the steps. Some moved off down the road, some squatted under a plum tree and began to wait.

Come in and take pictures, Emil said. *They left the bodies.*

Jack hesitated. *What?*

They left an object lesson.

Gray had already climbed the steps and was standing next to Emil. *It's not like you haven't seen a corpse before.*

Jesus, you two have become the fucking cryptic cops lately. Funny as hell, Jack said. He followed them into the house. Blood had dried brown on the wall inside the doorway. Bullet holes freckled each side. The body lay in a heap of rotting clothes. The bones barely held together by stretched, leathery skin. The bitter smell of rot was ghostlike, barely there. When the summer heat came, the place would reek. Jack turned away and looked at the rest of the room. All the furniture had been left.

This is my uncle, Emil said.

Gray took a picture. The click of the shutter made Jack flinch.

He put his camera away. *I think I've reached my quota of horror,* he said.

Gray reached out and put his hand on Jack's shoulder.

Come on. Emil led them into the kitchen.

How could anyone take two people on a tour of his home to show them the dead, decaying bodies of his family and hold back all his emotion? Jack wondered. The effort was making Emil sweat; Jack could see the drops of it slipping out of his hairline and down his gaunt face. He could see the tremble in Emil's hands.

In the kitchen was another body. An ax lay on the floor not far away. Jack glanced around, noticed there were no bullet holes here. *A "clean" kill,* he thought. *One or two shots.* The body twisted, collapsed in on itself. A pool of fluid, not blood anymore, dried on the floor. The bodies had been there long enough that the colonies of flies that would have swarmed like black clouds in the house had moved on to fresher breeding grounds.

The click of Gray's camera, and Jack flinched again.

Upstairs is worse, Emil said.

Jack lagged behind them, climbed the stairs as if his legs were barely able to support him. From the top of the stairs Jack could look either direction along the hallway. There were four rooms. Two to the right, two to the left. Emil and Gray entered the farthest one on the left.

When he stepped into the room behind Gray and Emil, he had to put his hand to his mouth. The body on the bed had once been a young girl, now bones and dry rotted flesh. The dried blood on the bedsheets told how she had been raped, the dried blood on the pillow and the wall how she had died.

My sister, Naza, Emil said. *She was sixteen.*

The sound of Gray's camera.

Jack kept his hand to his mouth and wanted suddenly to be home. He wanted to hold Nicole and Veronica and say he was sorry for being so selfish, so distant. Jack could almost calculate the ways his family could end up like that. He feared coming home to find them somehow vanished, to find he'd waited too long to say all he wanted to say.

He looked up to see Emil staring at him. So hard to tell what Emil was thinking. Something in his face had changed, and there were no tears. Silence in the room. Even Gray's camera became still.

I can't see any more, Jack said. *I'm sorry, Emil.*

He turned from the room and went downstairs, past the body and out the front door. He found a spot under a tree, away from the soldiers, and sat down. Tears pushed their way out and left cool lines on his cheeks.

There is fog in the morning, muffling Lian's senses. She is tired and stands against a tree watching Emil and Jack move farther away from her. She can't help but feel all of this has become ridiculous, and she can't quite believe Emil would be able to remember the places in the woods where he and Gray had been, or the place where they had been separated.

Already they have stumbled across four skeletons in the brush, bones turned white, and she has not been able to let the others know how detached from reality it has made her feel. How frightened. She wants to be out of these woods soon, away from the sound of the wind through the trees. The echoes of stories. The ghosts.

Lian crosses her arms over her chest, looks at the sky between the trees. She tries to keep herself ready for what might happen. Somewhere in this area could be Gray's bones. She doesn't want to find him by opening wallets and looking for his name but knows she must be ready to accept that some white skull in the ground is the one that once held up his face.

Lian, his letter began, *I probably shouldn't be writing this to you, but somehow, this place seems the best reason to suspend reason. I have come to Sarajevo to take pictures for the* Associated Press *and am staying at a* Holiday Inn*, of all places. It's surreal, certainly, and maybe because of that I could think of no one else to write to but you.*

I must be insane coming here, writing to you. Do you remember our quiet Saturdays before everything changed? It seems now that we barely talked about anything. It was as if there wasn't really a reason to. I was certain that each Saturday would be our last, but for a time there was always one more. Perhaps we should have made more of an effort to talk to one another, the way therapists say people should. But every time I thought that, it was while you were away from me. When we were together it never seemed essential. I could tell myself that everything would be told when it was time to tell it. I guess there was never a time to tell anything.

Slowly she slid the bedsheets off his hips and watched his stomach move with his breathing. She let her eyes go lower, down to what the sheet had revealed. Feeling his body in the dark did not create the sensation she felt looking at him in the morning sunlight. The dark had granted permission to be wanton, possessive, but in the sunlight while he slept, pulling back the sheet to stare at him became a transgression. It was a violation of some privacy, an act of objectification. If he had been an Asian man, she would have kept them both covered in that light, unmoved by the otherness of the body in her bed.

Gray's face was turned away from her, the tendons and muscles in his neck stretched tight. She touched him there first, lightly traced the cord of muscle disappearing into the center of his chest. His skin was warm, and she slid her hand down to the tangle of hair across his chest. She felt his heartbeat through the muscle and bone. *He's so thin,* she thought, her hand pouring across his stomach. She held his penis, soft and dormant. He moved then, his face turned toward her and his body shifted in her direction. She looked down at him, expected him to be awake, but his eyes were closed.

After a moment she took her hand away and laid her head on his chest. She felt his hand in her hair and closed her eyes.

When will you leave me? he asked.

Suddenly it was impossible to think, impossible to order the thoughts in her head. She had never wanted to think of that, had never let herself consider the possibility, but she had always known she would. She could never understand why she knew it, or why she couldn't shed the sense of obligation to her family, or where that obligation had come from. Her sister seemed so free of it. Lian didn't want to leave him, and so she never confronted those feelings. For brief moments with him, she could forget about her fears and immerse herself in the feel of his body next to hers, the sense of peace she found sitting next to him in darkened spaces. Talking too much would ruin it, chase it all away. It would change the bubble of silence they had shaped for themselves into a chamber of echoes. There would be confusion. Misunderstanding.

Let's not talk about that, she said.

Emil doesn't know how to tell them he is no longer sure they are in the right place. They have circled out from the clearing where the UN is excavating the mass grave, and it seems to him every tree is the same, every rise in the ground identical to the last, and behind every rise is another skeleton he is afraid will be Gray's. Then he will no longer be guilty only of betrayal but also of murder.

They have barely talked during the day, calling out to each other only when finding a skeleton. Each time Emil has hoped it would not be Gray, has hoped there is not a camera bag next to the skeleton. He wonders if there is any way Jack and Lian might come to think of him as a coward, or if they'll find out about the block of heroin still lodged under the seat in the car.

As the sun drops and the shadows begin to stretch out from the trees, he leads them silently out of the woods and back to town.

Emil stopped the vehicle, pointed to the spot the dog had run from. Jack could just barely see the small marker, pale green with white lettering, behind the low wall. They got out of the truck and walked over to the house and the walled yard. Jack hung back, taking the time to check his cameras, his rolls of film, and watched Emil and Gray climb over the wall.

It had been about a week since Emil's return to his family home. The strain of the situation seemed to show on him, and he was strangely distant with Jack.

Jack zipped up his bag and slung it over his shoulder, then followed them to the yard. The dog they had scared off had been digging at the grave. The tiny, mauled hand of a child rose up from the earth.

Fucking Christ, Jack said.

Emil lit a cigarette and knelt next to the grave. In the silence Jack and Gray stood as if in prayer. Jack let his eyes ease out of focus. Somewhere the dog barked.

I'm going to get the shovel, Jack said.

I think it's gone, Emil said.

We can't just leave this.

Her name was Fatima, Jack, Emil said.

Jack, her name was Fatima, Gray said.

Jack looked at the two of them, knew they were trying to goad him, to pull him back into their group. He just didn't feel like being there anymore. He was beginning to think he didn't have a role in the war these days, even as a witness. *Fuck you both,* Jack said. *I'm going to get something to rebury this child with.*

Jack, Gray said, but that was all Jack heard as he raised his leg to step over the wall.

He saw the holes appear in his pant leg, saw the blood mist out. For an instant that confused him. Then there was the sound of the shot, the faint crack reaching him at the same time his legs buckled under him. The lightning pain.

Sitting in the back of the car, Lian stares at the jagged skyline made by the mountains. The light is fading, and she thinks of Gray.

The car turns a corner and slows. She knows Daniel's shape intuitively. His back turned to the street, a woman beside him who watches the car as it moves past. The woman with him is unknown, but as her hand rises to the car, finger pointed, she suspects it is the woman Emil has talked about. Katja.

"We've been found," she says, watching Daniel turn to the street as the car rolls past.

"Who is the man with Katja?" Jack asks.

"My husband," she says.

"Well, this should be interesting," he says.

Lian slides down in the backseat of the car.

It is nearly dark when Daniel and Katja catch up to them. Lian has tried to figure out what she will say to him, how she will explain all of this. Every argument she imagines Daniel using includes returning to America with him, staying married. But it's not what she wants. She wants to find Gray, wherever he is, and stay there with him.

She sits in the backseat with the car door open, her feet on the rough asphalt, and stares at the ground. She touches the place on her shoulder where the scar is and rubs it like a charm. The first thing she hears is Daniel's footsteps, then the woman's voice. Now Emil's voice. Lian looks up and Daniel is standing a few feet away.

"Why did you lie to me?"

She looks at the ground again. "I didn't really lie."

"I'm not going to play word games, Lian."

"I certainly couldn't tell you the truth, could I?"

"Are you having an affair with him?"

"He was before we were married."

"Is he here?"

"No."

"Then why are you here?"

"To find him," she says and looks up at him.

Daniel clenches his jaw. The muscles in his face tighten and draw in his cheeks. She hates this look and gets out of the car, walks over to where Jack is standing. She knows this will infuriate Daniel even more, and she doesn't care. Emil looks suddenly stricken, tears on his cheeks.

"What's wrong?" she asks Jack.

"His cousin," he says. "Stjepan has died."

"Oh."

A hand on her shoulder just over the scar, a violent tug, and she feels her shirt pulled, the scar exposed.

"I am not done talking to you."

"Daniel," she says, tugging herself back from him.

"Is he the one who did this to you?"

"I told you you wouldn't want to hear this story."

"I want to hear it now."

She adjusts her shirt, looks at Daniel, then at Jack and Emil. The woman, Katja, is frowning, and Lian understands. She has come with the worst possible news for Emil, and Daniel is making a scene.

"We should go someplace where we can sit down," Lian says. "It's a long story."

Lian

Lian stood in the living room of Kay's apartment and looked down the hallway toward the closed bedroom door.

"Hey, we're going to be late."

"So what?"

Lian went down the hall and tried to open the door, but it was locked.

"I'll be out in a moment," Kay said. "You know where everything is. Get a doughnut."

"Yeah, right."

There was another voice, lower, whispering. A man's voice. Lian turned around and walked back to the living room. She sat on the couch for a moment, then stood up and paced around. There were muscles in her body that had never ached this pleasantly, and each twinge reminded her of the night before. She had expected Gray to want to study her like the photograph of a crime. But the moment they touched, she felt explored, even though he never seemed to open his eyes. Every part of her body had been studied with his hands, his mouth, his penis.

She had awakened in his arms that morning, sunlight spilling onto them through the window. It seemed they both put off his departure as long as possible. If it had been any other day she would have made him stay, but it was Sunday and her parents expected her at their house for dinner. As soon as he left, the doubts crowded in despite everything she had learned about him. Was it her, or was it the idea of her? Suddenly she couldn't be sure.

Kay once told her there were signs to look for with American men who had an Asian-girl fetish.

One, he doesn't ask you where you want to have dinner and just takes you to some Asian restaurant. Two, he assumes you prefer Chinese food anyway. Three, he has a lot of weird Asian stuff in his place. You'll know what I'm talking about when you see it. Figurines, paintings, all that shit that gets sold to tourists to satisfy their bland, generic ideas of Asian. Jesus, Lian. I know you've run across these types of guys before.

Yes, she had.

Lian heard the bedroom door open, then close, and finally Kay appeared at the end of the hallway.

"For once I wish they'd let us have a Sunday to ourselves," she said.

"Have to keep us under control until we're married."

"No shit."

Lian moved to the front door, then stopped. "Who's the man in there?"

Her sister smiled. "His name is Chris."

"Is he white?"

"No."

"Black?" she asked, but Kay only smiled. "Mom and Dad will lose it if they ever find out about that."

"Lian, you've got to quit worrying about them. If you try to be the perfect Chinese daughter, it'll kill you."

"I'm not trying to be the perfect Chinese daughter."

"When was the last time you didn't do what they wanted?"

Lian shook her head.

"If you put your foot down, they'll give up on you eventually, just like they did me," Kay said.

"No, they won't."

"See? Perfect Chinese daughter."

"Shut up," Lian said and went to open the front door to leave.

"Fine," Kay said, then turned to look down the hallway. "'Bye Chris. I'll be back in a few hours."

Lian wanted to tell her sister about Gray, but the prospect seemed to paralyze her. Such a sudden rebellion from her, she feared, could shock her parents far more than anything Kay had done. Maybe that was why Kay had always been so willing to do things: because Lian would always be there, dutiful and silent.

She tried to act normal at her parents' house that Sunday, but all she could think about was Gray. She could still imagine the feel of his hands on her skin, the feel of his lips where he had placed them. Standing up from chairs made her feel weak, and the muscles in her thighs and hips ached.

With so much in her mind, and the facade she tried to maintain, Lian barely noticed the reappearance of Daniel that day. She ignored

David and his arrogance. She sat quietly in her chair at the table and tried to give the impression she was following the conversation.

"You're not eating," her mother said.

Lian looked around to see who her mother was talking to. "Sorry, I'm not that hungry today."

"Did you eat doughnuts this morning?"

"No, Mom."

"Eat, you're too thin."

Lian looked at Daniel. He smiled at her slightly, more like a smirk. A conspiracy.

After dinner she found herself alone with him in the living room. David had left to return to Lawrence, and her father had gone to sit quietly in his study with a cup of tea. It was obvious what her parents' intentions were.

"What movies do you like?" Daniel asked.

"Well, *Breakfast at Tiffany's* is one of my favorites, and the book is good too. There are just too many to list, really."

"One of my favorites is *To Have and Have Not,* with Humphrey Bogart and Lauren Bacall."

"I haven't seen it," she said. "It wasn't one of Hemingway's best books."

"Are you more of a reader?"

"I suppose."

Again his conspiratorial smile, his eyes focused on something behind her so that she turned to look.

"Some friends of mine get together every now and then for dinner and classic movies. We're getting together next Friday. Would you like to join us?"

She looked at him for a moment. All the other men her father had dragged home to meet her or Kay had spilled their accomplishments as if they were on a job interview. Their cockiness had made her imagine them as the roosters that were used by families in Old China to stand in for men who couldn't be at their own weddings. A few could carry on conversations about something else, but not for very long. No one but Daniel had suggested getting her away from the family, or offered her something to do besides listening to his crowing. It was enough to almost make her think her father had finally taken some interest in her. Almost, but not quite.

"Perhaps. Call me later in the week," she said, but was already thinking of an excuse to not go.

When Daniel called to see if she still wanted to join him for the dinner party, she had just been told by Gray that he was going out of town for the weekend on an assignment. She was upset, and it seemed later that she had said yes to Daniel with a little too much enthusiasm.

The house Daniel took her to sprawled. The entrance was through a brick archway, overrun with ivy and lined by flower beds thick with plants she didn't know the names of. She let Daniel take her hand as they entered the house. The people he introduced her to were doctors. All of them single or in various stages of courtship with some other doctor. Their faces and names blended together, and she was afraid she would embarrass herself by calling someone by the wrong name.

There were nearly a dozen people, finally, who sat down to dinner. A few questions were asked of her about her job, how she had met

Daniel, and then the conversation wandered away from her and on to the hospital, to the dramas of their related lives. They didn't ignore her, but there was nothing for her to add to the conversation, no anecdotes to share.

Later everyone moved into the main room and spread out in front of a big-screen TV. Lian sat with Daniel on a love seat that had been pushed next to the large sofa. The movie was *Casablanca,* and Lian, like a few of the others, had seen it before.

She sat there with the same glass of wine from dinner and whispered the lines to herself in the dark. Occasionally she looked over and watched Daniel as his head sagged forward a bit, then snapped back. He yawned a couple of times, stretched, and finally looked over at Lian.

"I'm sorry. Long day at work," he whispered.

She smiled and nodded a little, then went back to watching the movie. After a while she looked over at him again; he had rested his head on the back of the love seat and fallen asleep. It was a little like being abandoned, she thought, but didn't mind. She got up once to go to the bathroom, and as she made her way through the group crowded around the TV, she noticed a few of the others had also drifted off to sleep. It was almost like an assemblage of the dead.

Daniel was still asleep when she came back. She settled into the seat as carefully as she could. When he finally lifted his head from the cushion, the movie was nearly over. She watched him push his glasses onto his forehead and rub his eyes.

"Sorry about that," he said.

"It's okay," she said. "The movie kept me company."

As soon as the movie ended, the party broke up. When they left, she let him take her hand again as they walked out the door and back through the archway.

He took her home and walked her up the stairs to her apartment door. They stood there awkwardly for a moment, and Lian knew he was hoping to be invited in.

"I'm pretty tired," she said. "I think I'm going to go straight to bed."

"Yeah, that might not be such a bad idea."

He leaned in to kiss her good-night, and she let him.

"I'd like to see you again," he said.

"You have my number," she said, knowing it wasn't strong enough to keep him away.

"Yes."

"Good-night then," she said and turned away from him to unlock the door. He was still standing there when she stepped inside and turned around to push the door shut. She smiled at him. "Go get some sleep," she said and closed the door.

"I missed you," Gray said.

"I missed you too," she said and rubbed her cheek against his damp chest.

She lay on top of him, her ear pressed over his heart, timing the rhythm, while his hands drifted along her back. The brush of a moth's wing. In the darkness she forgot to worry about the way he looked at her. All that mattered was the feel of his hands on her skin.

The heat trapped by the wet friction of their bodies was slowly bleeding off, and the moisture he had dragged out of her body dried between them. His smell had mixed with hers and changed. She breathed him in and let him go slowly.

"What are you thinking about?" he asked.

"Nothing. Everything."

Butterfly hands landed at her neck, and then his fingers combed through her hair.

"Why?" she asked.

"Just wondering what you were thinking about."

She lifted her head from his chest, looked at his face in the dark.

"I never know how to answer that question," she said.

"I won't ask it then."

"I didn't mean it that way. No one in my family ever asks that. I don't want you to think I'm being evasive."

"No one should expect to be told everything."

She placed her ear to his chest again and hoped that would be the end of his questions. All she wanted was to enjoy the feel of his long body beneath her and not dwell on those moments when she doubted what she felt.

There were times when they were together she would catch him looking at her, his eyes seeming to lose focus, as if he were drifting to sleep. The look could have meant anything or nothing. She always tried to assign it a meaning anyway. *Today it means he wants me. Tomorrow it will mean he is suspicious. Yesterday it meant nothing; he was tired.* She was aware of her inventions, aware of shaping him into whatever she needed to fit her mood. There were so many insecurities she would never admit to, even as she pinned him, naked, to this bed.

What she hated was his silence on some mornings. The distance he created, as if he were a continent she couldn't reach, his eyes focused on something always to his left. She hated the way he handled departures on those mornings, turning away at the door, saying his good-bye over his shoulder. She had tried to chart the source of those moments when he seemed to pull away from her. Could it have been something she said to him in the dark? A gesture not intended to be abrupt? Those distant silences seemed to enter him, secretly, in the darkness between lovemaking and the dim morning light.

She forgave him everything because she made her own fearful distances. A day sitting by the phone, wanting him to call but unable to answer when it rang. Her abrupt answers when he asked about her family. *I don't want to talk about them.* She erected walls to hide behind and scrutinize him from when it seemed she was about to be reminded of the differences between them.

She hoped the coming morning would not bring silence.

As if sensing her anxiety, he trailed his fingers like the edge of feathers along her back, then pressed them into her skin as if searching for something hidden underneath. He traced the bones of her ankles. Tickled her feet.

"Stop it." She laughed and pushed her legs out straight along his to get away from his hands.

He brushed his fingers along her ribs and under her smooth, damp arms. It made her squirm, and she pressed herself against the hard flatness of his chest, drew her legs up again to squeeze him with her knees. A flutter between them that could have been his stomach or hers. Finally she pushed herself up, away from him, so she sat across his hips and his erection bobbed against her belly. She reached down to hold it. Looking at him then, his body a dark shape against the pale sheets, his hands brushing her thighs, she was able to forget the tense silences, the doubts. There was only the feel of his body beneath her, his erect penis in her small hand like some delicate instrument. The sudden feeling of confidence it gave her to be able to effect change on his body.

She let go of him and reached to take a new condom off the night-stand. She tore the edge of the foil with her teeth, slipped out the condom and threw the foil onto the floor. Once it was on, she rose up on her knees to allow him inside. An involuntary sigh as she leaned over him, searching for his mouth with her own. She already felt out of breath.

"Slowly," she whispered.

He matched the small, slow motions she made with her hips. Soft, strangled moans formed and dissipated inside her. She used her whole body to squeeze him. Biting her lip, she tried to slow him even more and hold off the tremors she felt building up in his chest. She wanted to prolong its arrival so she could keep herself there in the moment of expectation. His hands clutched her tightly, and she sighed against his neck, pushed her hips down against him. It was sudden and hot. Everything seemed to pulse with red light. She imagined their bodies glowing in the dark like coals from a fire, slowly cooling to the blackness of sleep.

The morning sunlight woke her. She put on his t-shirt and a pair of running shorts and left him sleeping to go make coffee and collect the newspaper from the front step. She checked on him while the coffee finished. He was still asleep, so she filled a mug and went to the living room and sat on the floor with the paper spread out in front of her.

She laid each section flat on the carpet and stretched over it to read the articles that caught her attention. After she finished a section she would refold the pages and set it aside, front page down, so that when she was finished she could fold the whole thing up the same way it had arrived.

The click of a camera shutter jerked her attention from an article, and she nearly spilled coffee. Gray was standing in the hallway in his blue boxer shorts, his camera hiding his face. He worked the advance lever and clicked another picture. When he moved the camera away from his face, he smiled at her.

"What are you doing?" she asked.

"Wondering what you're doing."

"Newspaper yoga," she said. "There's coffee in the kitchen."

He walked behind her, eased himself down to the floor, and set his camera on the sections of the newspaper she'd already finished.

"Looks like there's coffee right here," he said and reached around her, gently taking the mug from her hand.

"Normally I'd fight you for it," she said.

"What do you want to do today?" he asked and handed her the mug before he reclined against the couch.

She leaned against him and looked at his legs. They made a tall triangle on either side of her, and with her free hand she smoothed down the dark hair on his left leg.

"It's going to be cooler today," she said. "Let's go take a walk in that park where that little stream cuts through."

"Isn't there a little deli near there?"

"I think so."

"Want to grab some lunch there along the way?"

"That sounds good."

"It does," he said.

The photographs he took of her were quickly hidden away in photo albums so her family wouldn't see them if they came by her apartment. The photographs she began to take of him also disappeared into the albums. She felt as if they were making a documentary of a secret, or that they had each become a visitor to a foreign country, photographing each other as if the other was a safari, or a war. Sometimes she imagined each photograph as a land mine she planted around herself, tempting someone to find it and set it off.

Her parents' disapproval of Gray, if they ever learned of him, was something she never doubted. When she was a teenager her father had forbidden her to keep the pictures of white celebrities she had cut out of magazines. When she went to her mother to protest, her mother only said, *All white men will think you're a whore.* With that in her mind, at school she found the smiles and looks from the white boys she liked were now suspect.

There were times when she wanted to study Gray like an insect under glass. How did he see her? What corners of his imagination did she inhabit, and what role did he give her? The fear that he would push her into stereotypes, make her into something she did not want to be, made her reluctant at times to let her guard down. It might be the moment when he'd say something, or do something, that would devastate her. *My little China girl.* A joke about Asian drivers. An inane question: *What is your ancient Chinese secret?* The fear that he would call her inscrutable, or say he couldn't read the expression on her face, as if her body itself was a foreign language he could never learn.

Lian wanted to be able to talk to Gray about everything. She wanted his mind spread out for her like a map, X marking the spot where all his secrets were buried. Fear bound her tongue to the roof of her mouth. What kind of damage would she cause if she made an issue out of something that didn't exist?

At times she could will herself to believe it didn't mean anything when he caught her withdrawing from him. Sometimes she would turn away from him after making love, and he would pull her back against him. Then, with his face buried in her long hair, his breath warm against the back of her neck, he would brush his fingers across her skin in slow swirls until she relaxed against him.

"Tell me what's wrong," he would say.

"Nothing, now," she would say, the apprehension dissipating like smoke.

She could never tell him what was bothering her. In those moments, she knew, there should be nothing wrong. The world he created for her was a cocoon against everything outside. She could dive into the circle of his arms, into the silence he created, and during the night all distinctions were wiped out. All that was left to her was the sound of his breath and the warmth of his body. The mysterious smell of his skin.

When they had plans to see each other, she would spend the day anticipating the smell of his body. There would be movements of the day lost to her, their precision left vague like a path through fog at night. She always hoped for their plans to fail so she could pull him onto the couch and press her nose into the fabric of his shirt. Warm her hands against his skin. She couldn't tell anyone how she sometimes wanted to bite into him, to devour him.

There were times when Gray was away from her, at work or out running errands or shopping, that another white man's gaze would destroy all her confidence in him. A stare, a hint of a smile that seemed too coy, and she would feel the way she had after that night during her freshman year of college.

Hey, China doll, the boy at the frat party had said, the smell of alcohol on his breath. His hand searched for the edge of her skirt. The music and the sound of voices loud enough that her first *No* was lost in the short distance between them. She pushed on his thick shoulders, raised her foot against his thigh. With the leverage of the wall behind her, she pushed.

Hey, China doll, what's wrong? She tried to walk out of the party, set on walking all the way back to her dorm in the chilly autumn night. She struggled through the crowd, the boy behind her. *What's wrong?* His hand on her shoulder even as she pushed open the front door and stepped outside. He was still behind her as she neared the sidewalk and the row of shrubs like shadows along the fence. Her heart began to beat faster.

She had not been a person to that boy but a curiosity. A fetish. Any girl from any Asian country would have piqued his interest. It just happened to be her that night, trapped there in the dark by a stubborn gate, a fence, the thick bushes, and a drunk boy who imagined her as something other than who she was.

The occasional fear of something horrible slipping out of Gray's mouth would make her conscious of the shape of her eyes and gnaw at her during his absences.

Hey, China doll, I hear you know things American girls don't.

It was as if she couldn't be anything but a caricature to some people. No matter what, she would be thought of as the quiet, submissive, and available Asian woman. She wanted to be free to try on personae like robes. Take them off if they didn't fit. She wanted the range of the white women she worked with but was sure it wouldn't be available to her.

Daniel, she was sure, saw her as a perfect Chinese girl. The inevitability of their courtship laid out for him like a diagram of the body. Start here, and you will end up married. There was no other choice. How Gray saw her was a mystery.

Over the summer months she began to feel like a circus performer juggling these two men. The one she wanted and the one she wanted to go away. It would have been so much easier to tell Daniel she didn't want to see him, but if he declined an invitation to Sunday dinner because she didn't want to see him, her parents would be upset. Instead she made as many plans as she could. She lied. Still he persisted.

On nights when she was alone, she would wake in the darkness of her apartment, thinking of the two of them. Daniel was everything she was supposed to want. He was gentle and kind. He could talk intelligently about so many things. But still, her interest in him was only friendly. Gray was everything she wished for and everything that was forbidden. His mystery couldn't be dismantled, and it covered a part of him she wanted to see.

She would get out of bed in the dark then, fight back her fears, try to ignore the ghostly shadows, and walk on cold feet out of her room to the kitchen for a glass of water. She would sit at the table and stare out the dark window at the flashing red light of a radio tower far away.

She wanted to sort everything out and put it in boxes in her mind like the bones in anthropology classrooms. Fragments to study and explain, to catalog and forget.

She would sit in her dark kitchen until her glass was empty, or until the sky lightened. Then she would go back through her dark apartment to bed. Sometimes she would sleep until her alarm clock went off, or until the sun tripped through her window to fall on the corner of her bed.

"***Are you*** going to marry him?"

Lian picked up her teacup, set it down, then looked around the small café where she'd met her mother for lunch. This was a continuation of the previous Sunday's dinner conversation during which her mother had, with no segue, asked, *When will you get married and give us grandchildren?*

"Marry who?" Lian asked.

"Daniel," her mother said.

"Doesn't he have to ask me before I say yes or no?"

"You could make him ask you. He's not asking because you give him the impression you would say no."

"Maybe I would say no," Lian said.

"What? You will end up an old mate."

"Old maid, Mother."

"That's what I said. It's hard to find a good man. Well, he's a good man. He also has family in Chinatown. We've not had family in California since Uncle William died."

"You and Dad could always move back there."

"Everyone is here, and Father is settled with his practice."

"Maybe I'll move away then," Lian said.

"You can't move. What about me when I get old? What about Daniel?"

Lian pushed her barely eaten lunch away and put her elbows on the edge of the table. She cradled her face with her hands and looked at her mother. "What about Daniel, Mom?"

"It was so hard for Father to find a man you would like."

"Why don't you push him on Kay?"

"We gave up on her. She is hopeless. I see how you look at Daniel over dinner. You have secrets from us."

"I never kept a secret from you before," she said and took her elbows off the table. She put her hands in her lap and bunched up her napkin. There was a paper cut on her right index finger, and she studied it. "Why would I start now?"

"You were always the secret daughter. You were always hiding things."

"And you think I'm hiding this supposed fact that I want to marry Daniel?"

"Yes. You don't want to admit that we are right."

"Mom," she said.

"Sometimes you just need a little push to do the right thing."

Lian stood up and placed her wrinkled napkin on the table next to her half-eaten lunch.

"I've got to get back to work, Mom."

"Fine, fine. I will see you Sunday?"

"Yes."

"Don't eat any doughnuts before you come."

"I don't like doughnuts, Mom."

Her apprehension expanded like a mushroom cloud. She watched as her parents convinced themselves a little more every Sunday that Lian wanted to marry Daniel. She began to wonder if she had given any signs that could have been taken as an invitation to that belief. But she couldn't think of one thing she had done. It had to be her mother. Her mother had to be saying things to Daniel when Lian wasn't around, asking him questions about the few times he had taken Lian out, convincing him Lian was falling for him but too shy to say anything.

On Friday night Lian locked herself in her apartment and turned off the ringer on the phone. All day Saturday she was surprised by the sudden sound of voices from the answering machine in the living room. Friends from work called. Telemarketers. Daniel. Gray phoned once from Texas, where he'd gone to photograph a baseball game, to say he would stay with the team for the rest of its road trip.

When Daniel called again on Sunday, she answered the phone.

"You're there."

"I've been ill," she said.

"Your mother is worried," he said.

"She knows where I live. She knows how to drive."

"What's wrong, Lian?"

"Tell them I'm not feeling well."

"Would you like me to make a house call?"

"If you want."

"I'll see you in twenty minutes," he said.

"Fine, fine," she said and hung up the phone.

She decided there was time to take a shower, if she hurried.

According to the practical expectations she'd grown up with, Daniel was the perfect choice. He was stable, had a good job, and was as dedicated to his family as he could be when half the continent separated them. The problem was that she didn't feel the things she wanted to feel when she was around him. She felt those things with Gray. There was the electrical snap that sensitized her skin when Gray touched her, the security she felt when he held her in sleep. It wasn't that she disliked Daniel or found him unpleasant. If they had met on their own, she was certain they would have become friends. Maybe more if there hadn't been Gray.

He knocked on her door sooner than she expected. There had not been enough time to get dressed after her shower or clean up the apartment. Dishes were stacked on the counter in the kitchen, mugs holding puddles of cold tea on the coffee table in the living room.

She tightened the belt on her bathrobe and tucked her wet hair behind her ears before she opened the door.

"You're early," she said.

"There wasn't much traffic."

She moved aside to let him come in, then closed the door.

"You really aren't feeling well, are you?"

"No, I'm feeling fine. I just don't want to put up with them today."

"Sounds like you really don't want to see me either," he said.

She shrugged. "The place is a mess."

"I don't mind," he said.

"Of course not," she said. "Sit down. Do you want some tea?"

"Yes. Tea sounds great."

She went into the kitchen and filled the kettle and set it on a burner. She knew something had been decided behind her back already or her mother would have been the one to call and scold her for skipping out on a family event. It wasn't the first time she'd tried to skip dinner. It was just the first time she'd come close to succeeding, and she couldn't help but think Daniel had something to do with it.

The kettle began to whistle, and she took it off the burner, filled the small teapot, then carried it and two teacups out to the living room and set everything on the coffee table in front of Daniel.

"I'm going to put something on," she said.

"Wait, please. If I don't say it now, I might not be able to when you get back."

She stopped and looked at him sitting there on the edge of the couch, his hands wrestling each other between his knees.

"It's okay, Daniel," she said. "Say it."

He got up from the couch and came to stand in front of her. His soft fingers touched her face, and she looked up at him. The expression was recognizable, obvious even. Its impact on her unexpected. She knew what he wanted to say and found herself divided between sympathy and fear. It paralyzed her.

"I'm in love with you," he said quietly.

"Daniel," she said, then stopped, the words suddenly dried up and gone. What could she say to him? If she simply said she wasn't in love with him, would he want an explanation? A reason? She would have to lie or tell him about Gray. And if she told him about Gray, it would be the same as telling her parents. Already there was a look of expectation on Daniel's face, its borderline relation to disappointment. There was everything in it. Her parents' hopes and expectations. Daniel's exposed heart. The only thing not there was Gray.

It seemed she stood there forever and silently hoped for Gray to miraculously appear and wrestle her away from Daniel and her parents. She closed her eyes for a moment to focus her thoughts, and Daniel kissed her. When he untied the belt of her robe and slipped his hands inside against her skin, she understood what was expected of her.

The next week went by slowly, and she felt controlled at times by some force outside her body. Daniel sent her flowers one day, took her to lunch on another, dinner on yet another. It was a struggle to act normally, and the effort erased the details of most things, but especially when she was with Daniel.

They had been talking at dinner. The details of the conversation were lost to her as nothing more than a hum until Daniel got up from the table and went to the restroom. In his absence everything snapped clear, and she looked around for a way out.

There were so many people in the restaurant, their eyes averted from her until she stood up from the table, clutching her purse to her chest like a life preserver. She made it as far as the front door, then, suddenly, turned to the pay phone by the hostess's station. She found change for the phone and called Gray but got the answering machine and hung up without leaving a message. When she turned around to look, Daniel had emerged from the small hallway that led to the restrooms and was on his way back to the table. She could see him looking around the restaurant for her. The door to the street was only three steps away, and she wanted to take those steps but could imagine her parents' reaction as clearly as if it had already happened. Her father's silence, which she had once wanted to break, would lock in place forever. Her mother would have proof, finally, that Lian was the daughter with all the secrets and lies even though Gray was probably the only thing she'd ever kept from her parents.

She walked back to the table and arrived at the same time as Daniel. She made up some story about leaving a message for her boss about something they'd forgotten to do at work. Daniel seemed to believe her, and then Lian's world slipped back into its blur.

After dinner Daniel took her home but had to leave right away because the hospital beeped his pager. He kissed her good-bye at the front door, and she let herself inside as he rushed back to his car.

The light on her answering machine flashed in the darkness. She went to it and pressed the play button.

"I've missed you," Gray's voice said. "I just got back into town. Call me, it's eight-forty-five and I'm home now, if that was you who tried to call earlier."

She picked up the phone and hoped the sound of his voice would make her feel better.

"It's me," she said after he answered.

"You don't sound well," he said.

"It's been a long week."

"Well, then I won't ask if I can see you tonight, but I do want to see you tomorrow. It's felt like the longest week ever."

"Yes, it has."

"We'll go to that park you like, with the fountain, then lunch. How does that sound?"

"Good," she said and let out a long breath. "It sounds good."

"But if you're not feeling well, I could just rent some movies and make you lunch there."

"No, I feel like I've been trapped in this place all week," she said. "Take me away from it, please."

"I'll come get you at eleven," he said.

"Ten," she said. "Ten would be better."

"Get some rest. I'll see you tomorrow."

In the morning, as she got ready, she struggled with what to tell Gray, or if she should tell him anything at all. *Things could still work out,* she thought. Maybe she just needed to tell Daniel she had given it a try, and although he was a nice enough man, it didn't feel right. But what would she tell her parents? That she was in love with a white man who made about as much money as she did? A white man whose parents had divorced? Her parents had always made it clear they expected Lian to marry someone from a good Chinese family, especially since they'd given up on finding someone for Kay.

Gray arrived right at ten, and she met him at the door. He kissed her and took her hand as they walked out of the apartment building. They hardly said anything at first. Gray drove and she sat in the passenger seat and looked out the side window, or looked at the hem of her red dress where it lay against her legs. The wind came in the open windows and blew her hair around, and finally she pulled it back and held it in place with a black clip she always carried in her bag.

Autumn was creeping in on the last of summer, although the temperature had already reached the 80s that morning. The leaves were turning colors on some of the trees. They walked away from the parking lot along the path that circled the entire park. She had left her bag in Gray's truck and didn't know what to do with her hands. She crossed her arms over her chest, then unfolded them and took the clip out of her hair. After a moment she gathered her hair again and locked it up in the clip. She could tell Gray was watching her, his expression made inscrutable by his dark sunglasses.

As they walked they moved aside for joggers and cyclists. By the time they reached the fountain Lian could feel the grit from the dusty path between her toes.

"I probably should have worn something else," she said.

"No, this is perfect."

They sat on the edge of the fountain, and Lian took off her sandals and put her feet in the cool water. She watched Gray as he undid his hiking boots and took off his socks. He got into the fountain and stood in front of her with his hands in the pockets of his shorts. It seemed he wanted to say something to her, but she could have been mistaken. It might have been her own wish to talk projected onto him.

There were other couples at the fountain, a few noisy children. It made the world around her feel much smaller. She stood up in the fountain, sloshed over to Gray, and leaned her forehead against his chest. When he put his arms around her, she heaved out a deep breath.

"That must have been one tough week," he said.

"It was."

"Do you want to talk about it?"

"Not right now."

"Come on," he said and bent down to pick her up in his arms. He carried her out of the fountain and across the bike path and up a small hill.

"Our shoes," she said.

"I'll get them."

He knelt and set her down in the grass on top of the hill, then went back for their shoes. When he came back and sat down beside her, she gathered up her legs and sat with her cheek on her knees. She looked back along the bike path they had walked down. Along the path, the morning shadows cast by the fountain, the trees, and lamp-posts were shrinking. She watched them for a while, imagined she could measure with her eyes the minute-by-minute evolution of their shapes.

There was movement beside her, and she lifted her head to see Gray stretched out on his back with his hands behind his head.

"It's going to start getting chilly in a few weeks," he said. "I always get kind of melancholy at the end of summer."

"Me too," she said and lay down perpendicular to him. She rested her head on his chest so she could look up at the sky. While he rested one hand on her stomach, the other played with her hair. The warmth of the sun and his gentle motions made her relax a little, and she closed her eyes.

It wasn't long, however, before the thoughts that had revolved in her head all week circled around and caught her. The night with Daniel. The fear of her parents' disapproval. She tried to push it all back, tried to concentrate on the slow glide of Gray's fingers through her hair. She wanted to curl up in his arms and cry. When he asked again what was wrong, she would tell him everything. But what would he do when she got to the part about Daniel? That, she knew, was the unforgivable part, and she knew she could never tell him.

"I'm not feeling very hungry," she said. "Can we just stay here a little longer?"

"Sounds like a good idea to me," he said.

There in the grass, looking up at the sky, she began to understand what she had been feeling all week. It was something like the feeling people get returning home from a long journey, where too many daydreams have materialized into a now half-remembered reality.

She tried to count back to when they'd met. Had it been late April? May? Had they only known each other about five months? It seemed so much longer, she told herself. She wanted more time to think and for everyone around her to stop pushing and pulling her in so many directions. But it felt as if her path had already been chosen, and fighting it would only delay her eventual surrender.

They stayed on the hill in the sun until the shadows pooled under everything, and then they walked through the park to the other side. Across the street was a little café where they had lunch. She kept expecting a conversation to spill out of them that afternoon, but the silence continued. On previous days like this, she had been thrilled their silences never became awkward, that they seemed capable of being together without chatter and reassurances. She had felt they could communicate then with just a look, or a touch on the arm, and guide the other somewhere they both wanted to be. It hadn't really felt like silence at all.

Now the silence seemed as heavy as a corpse, and when he finally took her back home, he hesitated at her door for the first time since they had met. She wasn't sure what to do with him anymore. If he went she could sort out her feelings, but then she'd be without him. If he stayed she'd have him to hold on to, but she would be aware of everything she didn't want to tell him.

She invited him in.

The silence lasted through the evening, and they fell asleep together on the couch. In the morning he woke her to say good-bye.

"Gray, what have you done with all the pictures we've taken?"

"I've put them in a portfolio."

"Would you ever get rid of them?"

"No, of course not. I'll keep them forever."

"No matter what?"

"No matter what," he said.

Lian expected it after dinner when they were cleaning, but it didn't happen. Daniel went with her father and David back to her father's study to talk. *Doctor business,* Lian's mother always called it.

With everything cleaned and put away, Lian went to lie down on the couch in the living room. She could hear her mother and sister talking in the other room but could not make out what was being said. Once her parents had given up trying to find someone for Kay, it seemed they liked one another more. Now all of their hopes were pinned firmly and relentlessly on Lian. For a moment she thought about slipping out of the house and driving to Gray's, but leaving would accomplish nothing.

Again and again she circled her thoughts until she could justify her decision to do nothing and hope everything would shrivel up like an unwatered plant. But things were happening anyway, and all she could do was watch. She placed the blame on herself for being a coward. She blamed Daniel for assuming she wanted to marry him and was only waiting for him to ask.

She should have expected this sooner. Her parents had trotted out opinions about Daniel and advertised him when he wasn't there. *He will make a good husband for someone,* her mother had said. *He is becoming very important at the hospital,* her father had said, and Lian figured it was the most he'd ever said to her that wasn't a lecture of some kind.

"Lian?"

She turned her face away from the back of the couch and looked at Daniel where he stood alone in the mouth of the hallway, his hands in the pockets of his slacks.

"Does my father want me for something?"

"No. Are you all right?" He took a few steps across the room and sat down on the couch by her feet.

"Yes. Just a little tired and . . ." she closed her eyes for a moment as her mother laughed at something Kay had said, "fed up with my parents."

"Would you like to get out of here?"

"What do you have in mind?"

"Anything you want."

"Do I have to make up my mind now, or can I do it on the way out of here?"

"I'll drive around until you decide."

"Fine, fine. Let's go."

The evening was cool, and she sat quietly in the passenger seat of his car letting the wind push against her face as he drove them along the highway, away from her parents' house. As long as he kept driving she felt she would be okay.

"So where should I take us?"

"I don't know. This is kind of nice, driving around like this."

"Then I'll keep driving."

Lian closed her eyes, tried to clear her head and not think of anything.

"What do you want most in life?" Daniel asked.

"I don't know," she said and tried not to think of Gray's fingers tracing a slow circle on her hip. "Passion."

"That's kind of vague."

"I didn't know I had to be specific."

"Let's stop here," he said.

Lian opened her eyes. It was the park where her company had sponsored the concert on the day she'd met Gray. She wanted to say *No,* but couldn't.

Daniel got out of the car, came around to her side, and pulled the door open for her.

"Are you sure you're okay?" he asked.

"Yes." She ignored the hand he offered to help her out of the car and stood beside him while he closed the door.

"Is it autumn already?"

"Just about," Daniel said.

His answer startled her, unaware that she'd said anything aloud.

The light was changing. There were streaks of red and deep blue in the sky. Pockets of shadows were forming under the trees and benches. He took her hand and walked with her across the grass to the empty band shell. The place where they sat smelled of pine trees and cut grass. Sunlight fell around them, touched their shoulders, and turned the interior of the shell red as fire. She wished she could walk into it, step from the point where she existed and fall into nonexistence. Burn away the confusion, the conflicting desires. Scorch the soft core of her heart.

Daniel was talking, his words tapping against her like leaves against glass. Faint recognition of the word *possibility.* The word *love.* She imagined her skin blackening and peeling away to reveal a second skin underneath, as ivory as old tusk and harder than stone.

"Will you marry me?"

She closed her eyes and turned toward the sound of his voice, opened them and saw Daniel's face. The engagement ring, already in his hand, hovered near her finger, ready to lock them together. She looked down at their hands, then beyond that to the ground.

It will be better this way, she thought and knew she had known her answer for weeks, no matter what she felt for Gray. *There are always things we wish we could do,* her father used to lecture her. *Then there is the thing we know to be the right and best thing to do.*

"I need to see you."

"You know I've been trying to reach you."

"I know, I'm sorry. There have been some things I needed to sort out."

"Are they sorted out?"

"Yes. That's why I need to see you."

"Tomorrow night?"

"Yes. At the little restaurant on Colfax. The Italian place."

"What time?"

"Eight."

"Lian, are you okay?"

"We'll talk tomorrow."

"That's awfully cryptic."

"I'm sorry, but please, tomorrow. We'll talk about it tomorrow."

She stood a little way down the street and watched as Gray went into the restaurant and got a table. She was uncertain what she would tell him, what she expected him to do. It was close to the time she'd said she would meet him, but she couldn't bring herself to step out of her hiding place in the entrance of the old shoe store and go down the street to the restaurant. The sun was nearly down behind the buildings, still holding back the night. The glare finally took away the view she had of him. She stepped out of the entryway and quickly crossed the street against traffic. She entered the small restaurant and went to his table.

"I'm sorry I'm late," she said.

"I was beginning to think you weren't coming."

They ordered food and a bottle of wine. Lian sat with her hands in her lap, covering the engagement ring with her right hand. She had wanted to look at him the whole time but found she couldn't raise her eyes to his.

"I've tried reaching you all week," he said.

"I've been busy."

"I figured, but . . ."

"Gray, please."

"I wasn't trying to make you feel guilty," he said.

She looked at her plate, looked at his hands where he held them like a prayer on the white tablecloth. She looked away at the shadows falling along the street outside. No matter where she looked, she knew he was trying to catch her eye, knew that when she did look at him she would have to show him the ring.

The food she ordered didn't interest her once it was delivered to their table, but the wine was good, and she finished what was in her glass and filled it again.

"Something's wrong, Lian."

"Yes."

"Aren't you going to tell me?"

There was a moment, a flash of defiance, when she nearly slipped the engagement ring off her finger and denied everything to him. Then it was gone, and she raised her left hand from her lap and placed it on the table. His eyes didn't move, but she knew he saw it.

"Have I just been recreation?"

"No, Gray."

"Then what?"

"Gray, it's better this way."

"What's better what way, Lian?"

"This way. He's Chinese."

"Oh, well, in that case."

"Gray, you don't understand."

"And I suppose I shouldn't want to understand, right?"

Lian watched him take sixty dollars out of his wallet and leave it on the table. It was nearly twice what the bill would have come to. Then he stood up. "I've had a truly enlightening evening. Thank you."

He didn't wait for her to get up from her chair, so she had to hurry after him. She wanted to reach out for his shirt and take hold. Let him drag her along to wherever he was going because that would certainly be away from here. Away from her family. He stopped outside the door, turned his head left and right as if he were lost, then finally took a few steps to his left.

"Gray, where are you going?"

"Home, Lian."

"Take me with you."

"What?" He turned to look at her.

"Gray, please. I can't go home to this tonight," she said.

She watched the passing of tension around his face, the struggle taking place inside him. He stepped toward her so suddenly she flinched, and then his hand was holding her wrist. They walked like that down the street to where Gray's truck was parked.

Her parents, she knew, would disapprove of him in so many ways. They would not like the old truck he was restoring piece by piece. They would not like his job that didn't pay any better than hers did. They would not like the shade of his skin, or the shape and color of his eyes, or the color of his hair. They wouldn't like the way he got excited when he talked about things he loved. They would not like the way he spoke. Her parents' brand of racism had been made clear many times. *We live in their country here, but we will not be like them,* her father always said.

He opened the passenger door for her, helped her up into the seat, and slammed the door shut with a force that made her jump. Lian stared at her hands in her lap as he walked around to the driver's side. She rubbed the engagement ring around her finger. As Gray drove to his apartment, the darkness around them thickened until she could barely see the ghost-like outlines of her fingers squirming against her thighs.

Things lined up in her mind to say to him. Each thought tumbled over the next, changed order with each subtle shift of her emotions. There was never this confusion with Daniel, never the combination of fear and desire. There was stability. He could touch her and she did not forget the time of day. His misperceptions of her were familiar and she could navigate around them; they were personal and small. She didn't want to be at the mercy of her desires. Then she wanted only that. She had grown up, it seemed, devoid of her own desire for anything, and those moments with Gray, giving in to some unfamiliar urge, had felt first like betrayal, then like an escape from prison. She could never decide, and in the end it was easier to trust what was familiar.

The truck stopped, and she continued to sit and stare at her hands until Gray came and opened her door and helped her to the ground. She had walked from this spot up to his apartment so many times. Her body was propelled forward by inertia, by the pressure of Gray's hand over hers. She waited with her head down as he unlocked the door and led her inside. He didn't turn on the lights, and Lian watched him lean against the door to shut it, his presence almost a shadow there.

"What now?"

"Don't talk," she said. She moved to him in the dark, pressed her body against his. Her lips touched his cheek, his chin, finally his mouth.

He pushed her away.

"What is this, a consolation prize? An apology?"

"This isn't an apology."

The words revolved in her head, and she knew she couldn't explain it to him. She had already said she was sorry. This was something else, her last act of internal defiance. She stepped back from him and began to undress. Gray's hands touched her waist, and she pushed them away and took another step away from him so he couldn't reach her as she undid the zipper on her skirt. Finally naked, she moved closer and reached out to undress him. Her narrow fingers wrestled with the buttons of his shirt. It took several tries to get the first few pushed through their holes. The pants were easier.

When she finally got his clothes off she placed her hands on his warm chest, and he trembled for the first time. She could feel his hands, palms moist on her hips, the tips of his fingers cool. Lian held her face against his neck, breathed him into her. The smell of oranges, a trace of photographic chemicals. The mystery she would later try to name.

She pressed herself harder against him, breathed at his neck, and felt his penis hard against her belly. Her hands slid down his arms to where he held her hips, and she stepped away, pulled him from the door. In the center of the room she stopped and pulled him down with her to the floor and laid him on his back. With him pinned to the floor she climbed over him, pressed his shoulders down with her knees, her hands in his hair.

He struggled free of her then and sat on his knees behind her. The gust of his breath touched her back, and she crawled to him, looking over her shoulder. There was something in his expression, even in the dark, that made her afraid. She nearly stopped and got to her feet, but then his hands were on her hips and he entered her. At that moment she couldn't tell who was more vulnerable, more likely to be devoured.

He rocked back and pulled her with him so she sat across his thighs. His arms, tight around her waist, forcing her down onto him.

He bit through the skin on her shoulder.

Her eyes closed against the pain and shock, and she strangled the scream in her throat. Instinctively she reached behind her, found his shoulder, and dug in her fingernails. She tried to get in under the muscle and pull it out. The thought, twisted and confused in the moment, was that she deserved this. She wanted the pain he was giving her.

She woke in his bed, his arms around her. The geography of her body confused by the proximity of his. The soreness she felt. Slowly she pulled as far away from him as she could without breaking out of the circle of his arms and looked at him in the morning light. His chest was the map of an invasion. The red lines of advance scratched across his landscape. It was hard to believe what they had done, harder still to believe the pain in her shoulder.

Gray didn't wake up when she broke out of his arms. Her thighs trembled as she stood. Other points of her body stretched against stiffness, and she went slowly across the room to the bathroom.

Naked in front of the mirror, she pulled her hair back to examine the mark on her shoulder. A jagged oval, black from the blood dried on her back. She took a washcloth from the towel rack and soaked it in warm water, then laid the wet cloth over her shoulder. The water in the raw wound made it sting, and she sucked air between her teeth. Squeezed her eyes shut against it.

She took away the washcloth and looked at herself in the mirror again. Bruises had formed along her ribs in the shape of his hands where he'd clutched her. They had tried to crush each other. She had wanted to be destroyed by the act, or destroy him. Yet there she was, with a warm washcloth in her hands and the knowledge she would have to go back out to him, ask him to take her to her car so she could continue this murder.

In his medicine cabinet was a bandage big enough, and she laid it over the wound, pressed it down firmly. When she took her hand away, a little blood was already seeping through the gauze. She left the bathroom and went back to the bed. He was still asleep, and she sat down next to him and shook him awake.

"I need you to take me to my car."

He didn't speak as he pushed himself out of bed and went to the bathroom. The four small wounds where she'd dug in her fingernails looked trivial, superficial. Lian turned her back to the door and sat staring at her feet, unable to get up again and go to the living room for her clothes. Next to her hand on the mattress was a spot of blood. Hers or his, she didn't know. She turned, looked at the sheets and the brown spots where blood had dried in the night. She tried to tell by the patterns whose blood each stain belonged to. *This isn't an apology.*

She turned away when she heard the bathroom door open, waited for his weight to move the bed. She felt him come across the mattress and wrap himself around her. His penis soft against her back, his arms around her waist. She flinched a little when he laid his cheek against her wound.

"I have to go," she said.

"Don't leave."

"Gray, I'll walk if I have to."

"Is he waiting for you?"

"Yes."

"Tell him to stop waiting. Tell him you've changed your mind."

"I can't do that."

"Why?"

She hated the feeling, like an electric shock in her eyes, before she started to cry. She wanted to get away from him, for only a moment, sort out her thoughts and find the best thing to say to him. At first she tried to push his hands away from her, but her strength failed. Her hands touched his and all she could do was trace the hard lumps of his knuckles. There was no way she could make him understand. It would always be like standing at a hostile border, and no matter how much he said he loved her, he would always be on the other side.

"I just can't."

"Yes, you can."

She broke free of his hands and stood up, turned to face him. She wanted to say it, but the words, the final leap into acting on the want, were too much for her. Her hands were cold, and she placed them on his face, moved her body close to his. He seemed so small then, broken, and she wanted to comfort him. But she knew of nothing to say.

Twilight

Daniel sits on a chair on the other side of the room with the photograph in his hands.

"And you never saw him again?"

"Once, when we were at the Plaza, he walked past us."

"I don't remember."

"No, why would you?"

"Why look for him now, after all this time?"

"You wouldn't understand."

"Don't tell me what I can or cannot understand." He can feel the others in the room watching them. "Tell me why you are looking for him," Daniel says.

"Because of what I did to him."

"Excuse me," Jack says and pushes himself out of his chair.

He leans on his cane as he crosses the room to the door. Emil and Katja follow him, and Daniel and Lian are finally alone in the room.

Daniel focuses on Lian and the calm way she stares back at him as if none of this were shocking or out of the ordinary. The photograph is bent in his hand, and the paper turns soft where the moisture from his fingers collects. Not sure how to navigate this moment, unwilling to believe the situation is as far out of hand as it seems to be, he tries to slow the beating of his heart.

"Are you telling me you love him?"

"Yes."

"Don't you think that if he were in love with you, he would try to get in touch?"

"I told him I never wanted to see him again. Why wouldn't he believe me?"

"That doesn't make any sense, Lian."

"Yes, it does. You just don't want to believe me."

Daniel stands and goes to the window. Outside, he can see Katja and Emil walking along the path from the boardinghouse to where the cars are parked. He watches them for a moment, then turns away from the window and leans against the wall. The things Lian has talked about seem overblown, dramatic. He can't understand why his wife seems to be talking of this man as if he were holy after leaving the scar on Lian's shoulder. He had wanted an answer, and now that he has it, he wishes he'd never known.

"Is there really something so wrong with our life?" he asks.

"It feels like a compromise."

He can't look at her and turns again to stare out the window at the sky, the slowly appearing stars.

"When we get home," she says, "I want to get a divorce."

In the silent room the air between them is still. He thinks that moving through it, making his way to the door and out of this horrible room he has paid to stay the night in, will make a sound like tearing cloth.

She hasn't moved from the bed, and he is certain her neck must ache by now, hung the way it has been for the last thirty minutes. The war inside himself, the dual desire to comfort her and to hate her, keeps him frozen by the window.

Who did this to you?

You don't want the answer to that question.

The order of secrets and evasions, the denials, the promises of future answers always pushed deeper into the future now seem like a script she followed. He can think of nothing significant to say, no course of action to take, except that he wants to go home and try to reorder his life. With or without Lian.

"A divorce will make our families very unhappy," he says.

"Are you saying we should make ourselves unhappy instead?"

"No. We've already done that. It's only a warning."

He rubs his eyes with his hands and finally pulls himself back from the window to sit in the chair again.

"It doesn't matter. You should have waited for me to come back."

"If you hadn't lied I would have trusted you to do so."

She moves, stretches out on the bed with her back turned to him. Part of the scar on her shoulder is exposed where her shirt has slipped down. Daniel stares at it. He had thought he could never do something like that to someone he loved, but now, with her saying she is set on leaving him, he believes it is possible.

In the room he has shared with the others for two days, Jack pulls the curtains shut. The gray light that had been trickling into the room was too much for him. Finally, in the dark, he sits on the bed, his back against the headboard, and takes out his flask. He can faintly hear Daniel's and Lian's voices in the next room.

The pain in his legs has moved from sharp to numb. He entertains the thought that walking so much has helped him, except he knows that once he returns to a more sedentary life, the pains will creep back.

There are so many things he can't remember about the day he was shot. How did bandages get put on him? How did he become suddenly surrounded by Bosnian soldiers, then by blue-helmeted UN troops? Somehow Gray's voice carried through it all. Maybe he imagined it. Maybe Gray was only there until the Bosnian soldiers carried him off to where the UN soldiers took over. Things were unclear, but for the last two years he has held on to the one thing he remembers: Gray's words before they loaded him on a helicopter to take him to away. *I'll see you in London, Jack. I promise.*

It had taken him months to get back to London. First he was flown out of Bosnia to a hospital in Germany, where he spent two months recovering from the surgery to save his legs. Months after that he had to learn to walk again. The steel shaft in his right leg and the plastic kneecap in his left were to be permanent additions to his physiology. The legs too damaged ever to hold together on their own.

Reluctantly he did what Veronica had wanted him to do and took the desk job with the news service. He spent his days picking over various photographs to be used with articles. It was tedious, and it seemed to him the younger photographers had no skill. He began to stop at pubs after work, get drunk before going home. Sometimes, as he walked to and from work, he would limp into traffic just to feel the adrenaline in his blood as cars swept past him. The shriek of their horns almost like rockets ripping the air. At night he would dream of gunfire and artillery.

He stopped talking to Veronica, stopped sleeping in the same bed with her. He was tired of the way she ignored him when he talked about the war, and all he could talk about was the war. As sick of it as he was, he couldn't stop it from being the first thing to spill out of him. He was tired of her accusations that he had abandoned her when she needed him to stay after her surgery.

They had begun to stalk the house for the absence of each other. Sniffed the air like animals. When they met, usually in the kitchen or the bathroom, they mumbled apologies to one another. There was the intense study of their own shoes until positions were changed on either side of the bathroom door, or until someone carried their meal out of the kitchen.

He had wanted things to be different, wanted it to be like it was when he'd come back from Vietnam. He wanted to be that young again and able to forget. They had once enjoyed the separation because returning was a drug in itself, and he'd always felt like he was falling in love with her again. But thirty years, her surgery and his wounds, had finally exposed other damages. Their lack of knowing.

He remembers the day when it all crashed.

Veronica handed him a manila folder.

What is this? He took the folder from her as if it might explode in his hand and opened it. *A divorce? Wasn't I supposed to get a lawyer as well?*

Yes, if there were anything to contest.

Veronica. He laid the folder on the table.

I don't want anything from you, Jack. I have my father's restaurant and the cottage. I just need your signature. I'm not putting up with this anymore.

When do you want these back?

Two weeks. Take some time to look them over, she said and left him alone.

From his bed in the dark room he can see his backpack, knows which pocket has his copy of the divorce papers inside. He imagines there must be a special psychological condition for someone who still carries a divorce decree around after the fact. He puts the cap back on the metal flask and tosses it against the far wall.

"***What are*** you going to do now?" Katja kicks at a rock on the path, keeps her arms folded across her chest.

"I am not sure," Emil says.

"There are very few reasons for either of us to stay where we are."

He laughs once, a brutal grunt, then shrugs.

"What are you afraid of, Emil? Being helpless in Sarajevo again?"

He doesn't say anything, and Katja stops, pulls at his arm.

"We can go to another country," she says.

"It is not that."

"Then what? Is it Mira? Do you think she will magically reappear at the house?"

"No."

"Do you hate me then?"

"No, Katja. I cannot talk about it."

"No. You will not."

"I do not know what to say."

She knots up her fist and punches his shoulder. He doesn't move, doesn't flinch, and it's like a switch being clicked over and she punches him again and again, a rhythmic thud against his arm. It's as if she wants to dislodge his voice, have what he can't say out in the fading light where she can face it, call it by its name, but he remains silent. Finally he catches her arms and holds her by the wrist. She seems unaware that she is crying. Slowly he lets go of her and gathers her close, holds her tightly.

When Katja finally stops crying she pulls herself out of his embrace and goes to sit quietly on the hood of Emil's car. When he reaches out for her hand, she pulls away. He doesn't know what to say to her anymore; his excuses, finally, have run out.

He looks away from her and out across the street. In the shadows he thinks he sees someone, but then the image is gone, fading into deeper shadows. *There are too many ghosts here,* he thinks. *Too many ghosts everywhere.*

"They need teachers in my town, Katja. There are still children."

"Yes, I know."

"We could get a place in the village and get rid of the farm."

"Do not tell me things I know you will not do."

"I cannot promise anything."

"Yes, I know," she says, sliding off the hood of his car. "You have not made one promise since the end of the war."

Katja goes to the car she and Daniel drove from Sarajevo and takes a cardboard box out of the backseat. She holds it out to Emil. He can't bring himself to touch it, and finally she carries it around to the front of the car and sets it on the hood.

"Did they say how he died?"

"Heart failure," she says.

"He was barely seventeen. How could he die of heart failure?"

"Maybe he willed it to happen."

Emil nods, then reaches out to open the box as if it were a bomb that might explode in his hands. At first the things inside are small and hollow of meaning. A few clothes and an old ball cap Gray gave to Stjepan. A comb. A lighter. A plastic film case. Emil peels off the gray lid, but it is empty. The last thing he removes from the box is a camera. It is battered but still seems to work. He twists the winding arm and feels a little tension. *There must be film still in it,* he thinks.

"Stjepan had this?"

"I suppose. They had the box packed when I got there."

Emil rewinds the film, then opens the back of the camera and drops the canister into his hand. He puts the camera back in the box.

The last of the daylight fades and the air begins to cool as he stands there for a moment, silently wondering why or how Stjepan came to have a camera in his room. Finally Emil carries the box to his car. In the darkness it takes him a few tries to find the right key to open the trunk. The things in the box are not things worth keeping, at least not to Emil. Even the camera. He is certain there were things in Stjepan's room that did not make it into the cardboard box. Someone at the hospital must have stolen them. He slams the trunk closed and shoves the keys into the pocket with the roll of film.

"Do you want to know why I will not return to Sarajevo?"

"Yes."

Emil takes her hand, leads her around the car to the driver's door. He opens the door and leans in to reach under the seat. The package of heroin is there, and he takes it out, drops it on the hood of the car. Even in the dark he can tell Katja is not sure what it is.

"Did you know that Goran is a drug dealer now?"

"No."

"Delivering heroin was the price for this car and enough money to bring Stjepan home in a wheelchair."

"Why did you not refuse to do this?"

"Because he wanted to come home and die. Because I knew Gray had promised to kill him if he were to ever become maimed, though Stjepan would not admit it to me." Emil closes the car door and picks up the package. "Go inside. I need to take care of this."

"Emil," she says.

"I'm not going to deliver it," he says. "Go."

She turns and walks away from him. He watches her until she has entered the boardinghouse, then he walks away from the car and across the road to the trees where he thought he'd seen the figure in the shadows. If the person was real he might still be in the woods, if not, it was simply a ghost. Twenty yards into the dark trees, with nothing around him but night and wind and the dead voices unlocked from the rustling leaves, he rips open the package and scatters the powder on the ground.

In the morning they pack their things into the cars they arrived in, wordlessly agreeing that the search is over. Lian refuses to ride back with Daniel.

Lian is still not certain if she wants to return to America. A part of her wants to stay in Potočari, continue to look for some sign of Gray. She could wait for the UN teams to uncover his body and mark it, even though she knows no one may ever be certain of the identity of anyone found in those graves.

Something still is not right, she thinks, watching the reflection of the small town slip away in the wing mirror, engulfed by the hills and trees. *Maybe Gray got out and went to France to be with that reporter Jack mentioned. Maybe he simply came back to America and decided to live in another town. Maybe he has been wandering.*

She turns to watching the road and the hills. Occasionally she glances in the mirror at Daniel and Katja in the car behind them.

The sunlight, a blanket of warmth despite the wind rushing through the open windows of the car, makes her feel drowsy. She closes her eyes and listens to the wind and the rumble of the engine.

I had a dream about you, she said.

Really? What happened?

You were a statue in a garden, and I tried to make you speak.

Did I?

No. Your face was always turned away, so I got angry and smashed you to pieces. But when I finished, you were still there.

It doesn't sound like a very happy dream.

No, she said. *Hold me tighter and talk to me.*

What do you want me to talk about?

Anything.

I had a dream about you once.

Yeah?

You were lost and I went looking for you.

Gray

It was dark when the first shells fell inside the Srebrenica safe area. Gray sat with his sleeping bag pulled over his shoulders and listened. He knew Emil would awake to the shellfire soon, if he hadn't already. They were sheltered inside a small shack that might once have been used for livestock. It was hard to tell.

"I think we have put ourselves in a tough situation," Emil said.

"How long have you been awake?"

"I have heard five shells."

"Me too. They seem serious."

"Yes."

"We should get moving, see if we can find out what's going on."

"Some morning," Emil said, "I would like to wake up to hot coffee and eggs."

They sat in the dim light, and Gray watched the red glow of Emil's cigarette cupped in his hands to keep it hidden. A habit one had to learn or a sniper would have an easy target.

Sitting in the dark, listening for the crunches of artillery, he began to think of Kansas. During his years at Kansas State University Gray would sit on the front porch of his apartment building and listen to the distant thunder of artillery from the practice range at Fort Riley a few miles to the west. The noise sometimes went unnoticed during a busy day, unheard if the wind were blowing. He never believed it was a sound he'd become intimately familiar with.

Most days now he woke up, grateful to be breathing, regretful that he felt safer because he knew he could pick up and leave if he really wanted to. It had been possible once, before coming to Bosnia, to go months without confronting mortality except in the abstract. An obituary in the paper, or a news story of murder, caused only a minor pause in his thoughts, a twinge of worry before life's white noise crowded back in. During his first forty-eight hours in Sarajevo he had learned mortality would confront him hourly. The pretty girl who smiled for a photograph while standing in line for water would have to sprint between buildings where people had scrawled PAZI SNAJPER on the walls with chalk.

"We should get in touch with the UN here," Emil said.

"I don't want to be stuck with them. I won't get shit if they insist I stay in their compound."

"You are taking a very big risk, Gray."

"I'm sorry I dragged you along."

Emil shrugged. "You did not force me."

They collected their few things and crawled out of the shack. Outside, the fog was thick. The sound of artillery and rifles came from southeast of the enclave, distant and erratic. The faint sound of engines could be heard everywhere. They entered Srebrenica through the woods and hills, through burned-out buildings. They avoided the roads.

As a child, when Gray had imagined war, it had always been fast. His daydreams were fed by movies and grainy documentaries. He imagined combat would flash out of the blue sky like lightning, then vanish. Maybe, in some wars, it had, but this war was like a deadly chess game between pensive masters. The Serbs would make a move, then wait to see how the UN and NATO would react. Then, when it seemed nothing would be done, they would move again. The Bosnians, outnumbered, poorly armed, would try to position themselves behind the UN troops, knowing that certain battles were lost unless the UN called in air strikes or actually engaged the Serbs on the ground. It almost never worked.

"We are lost without Naser Orić," the man said. "The Serbs are not afraid of us now that he is gone."

Emil translated, but Gray was able to get most of it.

Things had been deteriorating fast over the previous eight hours, from what Gray was able to gather by talking to the fighters. The Dutch UN troops had been pushed out of several of their observation posts. Bosnian civilians had begun to arrive in Srebrenica from the towns in the southern parts of the enclave. Thousands of people were being crammed into a village that had not had running water or electricity for years.

"We wonder why the UN does nothing at the right time," the man said.

Gray nodded, spoke to the man in Bosnian: "I do not know either."

"You will take pictures of what will happen, yes? Show all of the people in the world how we are slaughtered animals and the UN does nothing because they think we all want to be martyrs in a holy war."

Gray did not understand all of it and looked at Emil. He translated.

"I will take pictures of the truth. They will be ashamed of themselves."

The man nodded. "But not until after my family is dead."

"I come from a sleeping people," Gray said.

"You are awake," the man said. "I must get back to my family."

Gray sat quietly and stared into the burning coal of his cigarette. He was aware of Emil across from him, jabbing a stick into the ground like a knife.

"I should have stayed with the Krajina brigade after Jack was shot," Emil said.

"They're not here."

"I could join the fighters here."

"I don't think they would have a rifle for you."

Emil laughed quietly. "They might have a rifle. It would only have five bullets."

"Look, Emil, the way things are going, I don't think we should put ourselves in a situation to be corralled with the Bosnians either. Understand? I have a feeling that most of those people will not get out of here."

"Only a feeling? I know that none of them will get out of here unless they are very, very lucky. Are we very, very lucky?"

"I hope so."

He was awake in the dark, and the fighting, for the moment, had quieted down. It was difficult not to think of her.

There is nothing in the dark that isn't there in the light.

Yes, there is, she said. *There's my imagination.*

After Lian had left him to marry that other man, Gray couldn't sleep without a light. The darkness would pry open his eyes, and he would stare into shadows. He imagined disrupting the wedding, arriving to take pictures and then confessing himself to the assembled families. After that he was never sure what might happen. What would fill that silence? He tried to fill it, force some conclusion onto the imagined blank moment, but everything felt fake, contrived, borrowed from movies and old books he'd read. And in that cul-de-sac of his imagination, his mind still tripped over that heartbeat moment when he'd bitten into her skin.

Gray became fascinated with damage.

The police scanner he had rarely used before was on continuously, and he would rush to car accidents, nearly adding to the list of victims. He would shoot rolls of film over the tragedy. All of his pictures seemed to be of black blood soaking into the white foam of ripped-open seat cushions. Always the aftermath, never the victims themselves.

After Lian's engagement was announced in the paper and he knew the man she'd chosen over him, he imagined he would be in an accident, be rushed to the hospital. His body reassembled by the man who'd helped destroy him.

Gray's world became macabre. Silent. He muted the television and looked for news of war. And there was Bosnia.

The war unfolded like a horrible movie. He watched the reports on television, wondered what it would take to get over there if the newspaper didn't want to send him. He imagined himself taking pictures amid the flying bullets and the scream of shrapnel.

He saw her wedding announcement as the paper was coming off the presses and read the details of their wedding. He went out and bought a card, bit off one corner, and mailed it as the delivery trucks rolled off with the newspapers, knowing she would not see it until after the honeymoon.

A few weeks later he saw her on the Plaza, walking with the man she'd chosen over him. He passed Lian slowly, her husband oblivious to the fact she was no longer paying attention to him. Gray brushed the back of Lian's left hand with his, then looked back once at her receding face.

Emil's voice in the darkness. Something Gray didn't understand.

"I said it is going to be dawn soon. The shelling will start again."

"I didn't get much sleep," Gray said.

"You do not ever seem to sleep well."

"I must, or I would be crazy by now."

"Or you are so crazy you do not know you are crazy."

"That's why I like you, Emil. You've got a shitty outlook on life."

He waited for the shells to fall and tried not to think about Lian.

The edges of his consciousness pulled down so he could focus on just the last few years. His time without Lian, his time in Bosnia, then in Amsterdam and Paris. How Suzzette had tried to work her way inside him. She had wasted no time dragging him up to her room in the Holiday Inn. *I will fuck her out of your system,* she had said to him. But in the dim halo of candlelight, her dark hair had made him think of Lian, and so he had lied. *Yes, she's gone.*

Suzzette was nearly his first casualty. As they huddled together in a building near a dangerous neighborhood, a sniper's round shattered her cameraman's head. Blood exploded out of his body. The dead man fell against Suzzette, sent her sprawling to the ground. Gray thought she'd been shot, and in the confusion and panic he pulled her into a corner of the building, wiped the blood away from her face, and called her Lian.

She left the next day to take her cameraman's body back to France. *Look me up when you get her out of your system,* she said and gave Gray her address in Paris.

His appearance at her doorstep months later had been a surprise. Suzzette's life, as he'd expected it would, had moved on despite what he'd hoped for. She put him up in her guest room, and he told her stories about things he'd done with Emil and Jack. Made his first plans to return to Bosnia.

Be careful, she told him. *If you need anything, write or call.*

Gray followed Emil as they slipped out of the empty house and made their way through the woods, a few yards from the road, toward the sound of fighting. The Serbs were pressing the Bosnians closer and closer.

I'm losing it, echoed in his head. The idea of shell shock blossomed, faded as he watched Emil leading him forward. *If he can live this life, I can.* His feet hit hard against the ground, shaking loose the sweat from his skin. His mind was focused not on following Emil but on an expanse of bedsheets and unseen cool hands in the dark, warming themselves against his chest. The sound of his own name spoken softly in his ear.

His name screamed in his ear and hands shoved him to the ground. The sound of rifles. He stared up at the overcast sky, the milky sun barely making its way through the cloud and fog.

"Were they Serbs or Bosnians?" he asked.

"Bosnian, I think," Emil said. "I hope."

"Shit."

"Gray," Emil said, then stopped as a pair of men with rifles appeared out of the trees.

"You should not be here," the man said. "All the civilians are in the town square."

"Press," Gray said.

The man laughed. "Did you get bored with the women and children?"

Orders came to the group they were with by messenger, a young man barely able to grow a mustache. Gray listened to him talk to the commander and picked up bits and pieces of what the boy said, then asked Emil for clarification.

"They're going to try to break out to the north. The army will spearhead the column. A few of them don't think it will work, and they are going to try to find refuge with the Dutch troops."

"Yeah, I got most of that. What else?"

"The platoon we're with is going to be part of the rearguard."

"Bloody hell, that'll be good."

"I think," Emil said, "we should try to move farther up the column."

"Why?"

"Safety. Protection. No one wants to be the rearguard in Bosnia."

"Think of the pictures, though."

"Are you going to keep your head on the job?"

Gray looked away from Emil and out at the dim sky, then down at his hands.

"How do you keep from thinking about her all the time?"

"I remind myself that the only way I can learn what happened to Mira is to keep myself alive."

"You are certain she's alive then?"

"No. But what else do I have to hope for?"

Gray nodded. "I will keep my head."

The messenger stood over them, his head tilted to the left. "You are American," he said in English.

"Yes," Gray said.

The young man sat on the ground across from Gray, laid his rifle across his knees.

"Before the war my parents were going to send me to America to go to university."

"Which one?"

"We had not decided yet."

Gray looked at him for a moment. "What's your name?"

"Fikret Hasan."

Gray took out his notepad and wrote down the name. "Are your parents still alive?"

"No."

"Here then," he said and wrote down his own name and Suzzette's address in Paris. "When this war is over, contact me here. I'll see what I can do for you."

Fikret shook his head. "I would lose it, I am sure."

Gray shrugged. "Take it anyway. I have your name, and I will try to find you. Put it deep in your pocket."

The boy took the slip of paper and stuffed it into one of his pants pockets.

"I will see you around," Fikret said.

"I do hope so," Gray said and took out his camera. He snapped a picture of the young man as he stood over them with his rifle cradled in his arms.

Gray stood on a hill, hidden among the trees, and looked down at the town of Srebrenica. It seemed there were thousands of people crammed into the market square. A few blue-helmeted UN soldiers moved around. Farther away the growl of tank engines. He had spent all his time thinking it would be better to be away from the crowds and the UN forces, but from the vantage point above the city, he changed his mind. The breakout would happen, or it would not, but the civilians, desperately clinging to the mercy and safety represented by the crippled UN, would be the ones with the deepest story to tell.

Gray tugged on Emil's sleeve. "Emil, these guys are breaking out on their own. They're deserting."

"I told you; no one wants to be the rearguard. Happens all the time. Live to fight another day."

"I want to be down there," Gray said.

"How good is your Serbo-Croat?"

"What?"

"Gray, this valley is going to be slaughtered. I can't go with you down there."

"If they're deserting, then down there is where the story is, Emil."

"For the people who aren't involved in the war. Story I want to hear is 'Hello, Emil; I've missed you so much. I love you.' Not some Chetnik telling me to put my hands behind my head and say hello to Allah."

"I'm going down there," Gray said. He watched Emil's face; watched his jaw tighten and the creases around his eyes deepen.

"I will see you around then."

It was easy for Gray to slip back into Srebrenica, find his way to the crowd of refugees who'd come from the smaller villages and gathered in the town center. He stayed on the periphery, taking a few pictures of the people. Their gossip washed ashore at his feet. Some said the Dutch UN troopers were going to swap the refugees for their secure passage back to central Bosnia. Some said the Dutch promises of NATO air strikes were lies. They all believed they were being left to be slaughtered.

He ducked down alleys and into buildings to avoid the Dutch troopers. They would pull any journalists into their compound to protect them, and there would be no more true pictures.

Some of the people told him they would try to get to Potočari, a few miles north of Srebrenica, where the Dutch had their headquarters. From there they weren't sure what would happen. Maybe the Serbs would stop; maybe Naser Orić was bringing the Black Swan brigade to their rescue. Or maybe they would simply flee for central Bosnia.

In the evening he found a building a few streets back from the market square and hid himself in a back room. One tiny window up high on the wall let in silvery light. He lay on his sleeping bag and smoked a cigarette, listened to the occasional crash of artillery. The spurts of small-arms fire like mutant crickets. He hoped Emil was doing well, but he wished Emil had come with him so he would have someone to speak to in the dark. Instead he lay awake with his back pressed to the wall and stared up at the tiny glowing window.

You look *tired, Gray.*

It was a shitty day.

He came into her apartment and dropped onto the cushions of the couch. The muscles in his legs and arms felt hollow, drained. He let his eyes close as Lian walked across the living room, then he felt her weight sink into the couch next to him. The smell of her body was like the arrival of spring. He felt her hands, warm this time, touch his arm, his forehead.

I guess you don't feel like going out then.

I'm sorry. I almost called and canceled tonight.

Why didn't you? I wouldn't have minded.

I had to see you.

She folded him in her arms, and they sat quietly on the couch.

Why do you never ask me what I'm thinking about?

Would you tell me? she asked.

Gray frowned. *I'd try, but I don't think I'd ever get it right.*

Then what's wrong?

I was just wondering.

She pulled her hair back, twisted it, and draped it over her shoulder. She rested her head on his chest, her hand on his right thigh.

It was something that was never asked in my family, she said.

Really? Jesus, my family seemed to ask it fifty times a day, and I was the only one who ever shrugged and said I didn't want to talk about it.

The black sheep.

The troubled sheep. My dad put me in therapy when I was sixteen.

Did they cure you?

I think I put the therapist in therapy.

They were silent, and Gray listened to her breathing, concentrated on the weight of her hand on his thigh. He knew there were so many ways to be dysfunctional, to chew up another person and make them useless, demanding a partner to be a certain way when she can't, or never being pleased by each other's attempts to reach common ground.

He felt her body shift with her breathing, her hand twitch on his thigh. He wondered if they could fill the gaps in each other, if they could prop up the places in danger of collapsing. He laid his head back against the couch and finally let himself fall asleep.

Gray smoked another cigarette and tried to think of something other than Lian. He would need to move with the refugees in the morning, find a way to hide himself among them so he could get the pictures he wanted and not be herded into the compound with the Dutch troops and their hangers-on.

But his mind circled Lian. Her gravity, even removed by time and distance, by those weeks in Paris with Suzzette, pulled him to her like a moon, trapped. He wanted that severed, wanted to drift away from her and slowly forget the feel of her hands, the smell of her hair, the way she looked in dim light, her black hair making her pale skin as brilliant as trapped lightning.

He had wanted this war to jar him loose from her. He'd wanted this war for other reasons, childish reasons. To be heroic. To test himself as a man and find his breaking point. Before he'd started across the wilderness to Srebrenica and the safe area, he had wondered if he'd reached that breaking point and not noticed. Wondered then, in his dark room with the high, small window, if he'd been broken and was simply falling through the world waiting to crash. Shell shocked and walking into his coffin thinking it was a taxi to the other side of town.

Would you tell me your dreams?

Are you going to interpret them?

No, Gray. Not those dreams. I meant your hopes.

Well, I guess I . . . I guess I don't really know for sure. I'd like to be a husband and father someday, but I don't want to wake up twenty years after getting married and realize it was a mistake. And there's that picture thing. I want a picture that has impact, right in the gut.

What else? She smiled.

I think that's it, Lian.

Gray lit another cigarette and thought that, if he could have found the courage to say *I want you, forever,* it might have kept her from leaving him. His body ached to sleep, but he couldn't shut his eyes for more than a few moments before the memories crowded in and pried him awake. Then there were the shells exploding from time to time. It was as bad as when he'd first gotten to Bosnia, snapping awake in his bed in the Holiday Inn at each burst of gunfire, each dull crunch of a mortar round exploding.

He needed to sleep. If he wasn't alert the next day or the day after that, it would be ugly. Tragic. Did he want that? There was part of him obsessed with the idea that dying here would be acceptable, that maybe he wanted to be tragic. No one knew all of the story, though. There was no great-minded narrator following his path with a string of elegant words. He would pass into death the way ether slips into lungs.

He smoked the cigarette down to the filter, and somewhere between flicking the butt away and reaching for another, he fell asleep. In the morning it would seem to him as if nothing had happened, his mind had carried on with the process of taking another cigarette, lighting it, and smoking, but his body had shut down, curled there on the floor with one hand stretched out to an empty pack of cigarettes.

He woke to shellfire and the clatter of rifles. An empty stomach. The dream of a last cigarette.

He and Emil had not planned this well. The food they'd carried with them had run out days ago. Gray sat against the wall and listened to the fighting in the hills, the uneasy wash of voices from the crowd in the city. He tried to find some part of himself that would get him to his feet and out of the building, but he could only sit. His head dropped forward onto his arms where they were folded over his knees. He was awake, but it felt as if he had never slept, not once in his life.

There was an explosion close by, and then screams.

He had to move. He pushed himself up, pulled on his nearly empty backpack, and left the building.

When he reached the sea of refugees he could see the blue-helmeted Dutch troops loading wounded into trucks. As he moved around the edges of the crowd, he took pictures. He wanted to get closer to the wounded being evacuated but was sure the UN troops would see him. A few of the women were already starting up the road to Potočari, a few of the men slipped into the woods. He would have to decide between following the women up the road, exposed to anyone hiding in the woods who might want to shoot him, or going into the woods to see what might happen to the men. The only problem was that in the woods he didn't know his way around, but he could at least make an attempt to hide if he needed to.

He went into the woods.

Gray took a moment to get his bearings. The road the families had taken headed northeast, and the others had headed into the woods going northwest. There were two stories, and he had to decide which one to follow: the ones to the northwest fighting their way out, or the ones to Potočari falling back with their children and hoping for protection from the ineffectual UN troops and NATO air strikes that had yet to materialize. He decided to follow the families, so he slipped into the woods and headed northeast.

There were already dead in the woods.

With nothing to protect him, no one to guide him, he held his camera and hoped it wouldn't appear like a gun, hoped it might ward off the bullets and knew it wouldn't.

He wanted a cigarette, to sit down and rest. The smoke would push the scent of death out of his nose. A good rest might take the tremble out of his legs. But if he rested, he might not make it to Potočari before night. In the dark his chances of running into the Serbs were doubled.

In the air around him it seemed as if the firefights shifted location with the wind. The sound of automatic weapons came to him from all directions. His back tingled, and he kept turning his head to see if he was being followed, or if there were rifles pointed at him. At times he felt certain he'd lost his way, and he would stop, try to get his bearings in the woods by looking for the sun and where it made his shadow on the ground.

The man with the rifle appeared in front of him. Gray absorbed everything in the heartbeat it took to stop. The man's body rose from behind a cluster of dense shrubs and came forward. The small black hole of the rifle barrel was leveled steadily at Gray's chest. Fatigues, a badly fitting beret, dirty tennis shoes. A patchy thin beard. He was just a boy.

The boy spoke slowly in Serbian. "You are a journalist?"

"Yes."

"English?"

"American."

"You should not wander around like that here."

Gray did not respond, stood with his camera held to his chest. A shield. The soldier lowered his rifle from his shoulder.

"You could photograph something for me."

"What?"

"A party." He turned his head slightly and swung his chin in the direction of a clearing behind him. "Go that way."

Gray moved past the boy, who followed him. He knew the rifle was pointed at his back. It was best to go along with the boy and play the game. As he stepped out of the woods and into the clearing, he wasn't entirely surprised by what he found there. Four other boys in uniforms surrounded a woman who was bound at the wrists and curled on her side in the dirt.

"She is *torbari,*" the boy said. "She has killed many innocent Serbs in the villages around here, slaughtered them in their beds after fucking them, then stolen their crops and their livestock."

"I do not know that word, *torbari,*" Gray said.

"Torbari?" The boy looked at him, then took hold of Gray's camera bag and tugged at it. "They are bag people, looters, thieves."

One of the boys laughed. The sound was nervous and uncomfortable. Gray stood and stared at the woman's bound wrists. The weight of his own body seemed to press his feet into the ground like the roots of a tree.

"You will take pictures."

"No," Gray said.

The boy drew a pistol and pressed the barrel to Gray's head. "Do you think they will miss you right away?"

Gray stared at the woman's hands, unable to meet her eyes. She was silent and still. It made Gray wonder if she was already dead, or unconscious. He closed his eyes and found he was more afraid for himself, and ashamed.

"I will take pictures."

"Take the pistol," the boy said to the one who had laughed. "Make sure he is taking pictures."

Gray opened his eyes and looked into the woman's face. She was alive, she was awake, but something was gone. It was as if she had given up struggling long ago. She knew what would happen to her, and she had prepared herself as best she could, pulled back into the depths of herself. The black emptiness of her eyes stunned him. The boys were making a mistake. Gray knew it; the woman knew it. In their arrogance, their sense of invincibility, they were going to let him document the crime, and all he needed to do was get the photos out.

They cut away her clothes with a knife. She tried to fight them a little, then one of the boys pulled her bound arms over her head, and two others held her legs open. The boy that had stopped Gray in the woods took down his pants and held his erection in one hand as he put himself between the woman's legs. When she continued to struggle, he slapped her face hard. Blood appeared from her nose.

"If you fight it will take longer," he said.

She turned her face away, and Gray could see tears. He felt like vomiting, but there was nothing in his stomach, so he took pictures.

The boy who'd laughed held the pistol on him as all the others took turns with the girl. It was as if he'd been forgotten. Gray was certain they would take the film out of his camera in the end, but he hoped none of them would notice he'd shot three rolls, hiding two in the huge pockets of his vest.

After they were finished the one who'd stopped him led him back into the woods. He yanked the camera out of Gray's hands, fumbled with a few of the knobs.

"If you open it right now you will ruin the film," Gray said. "Don't you want your keepsake?"

The boy popped open the back of the camera and stripped out the film, then threw the camera to Gray.

"Walk fast."

As Gray walked away he heard a shot. He wanted to sit down, cry into his hands. He wanted a gun so he could put the hot barrel to their heads and shoot them. Instead he stumbled through the woods toward Potočari.

He arrived at Potočari in darkness, guided by the sound of fighting and by the muffled sound of thousands of refugees. Trucks driving to and from the town led him to the battery factory where the Dutch battalion had its headquarters and where the Bosnian civilians had gone seeking their last chance at protection. He found an entire city crowded into a field between the factory and the first buildings of the small town. Already the smell made his eyes water.

People slept propped against each other, taking care not to fall in the smears of their own excrement around them. Gray stood on the edge of the mass of people, his hunger uncut by the noxious smell. There was not much ground to cover to get to the gates of the Dutch compound, but there was the pressing sea of people. He would have to walk through them to the gate to present his press credentials. The uproar at his passing, he was sure, would start a riot.

He turned and slipped back into the woods. He climbed a hill in the dark, unconcerned with whom he would encounter, and turned to look down on Potočari. Even in the darkness he could see the crush of people, a dark ocean washing up against the walls of the old factory. The shores of other buildings.

There was nothing to concentrate on except the tight, hollow feeling in his stomach. The trembling in his arms and legs. His head felt pinched and drilled into. The face of the captured woman kept shifting through his mind, turning into Lian, turning back into her own. Everything seemed to circle in and flow out from those eyes. The screaming silence around her. He stumbled farther up the hill, feeling dizzy and light-headed, but he kept trying to climb.

Exhausted, he stopped moving, and his body collided painlessly with the ground. He dreamed that the woman walked in circles around him, her body washed clean, white as moonlight. Voices surrounded her, came out of her body, out of the sky and stars that shrouded her and collided with him and rolled him along the ground in the dark.

He woke to water in his mouth, a hand at the back of his neck. There was the diamond-like sparkle of sunlight through trees.

"You chose the right hill to climb," Emil said. "You are the luckiest man I know."

Gray swallowed, tried to push himself up.

"A few of my comrades found you last night," Emil said. "You are dehydrated."

"Yeah," he said. His voice soft, barely falling past his lips.

"Here." Emil gave him a few plums. "There is an orchard nearby, but only the highest branches have fruit. I have a little more food. Not much. I will be back in a moment."

Emil left him a canteen. Slowly he ate the plums, chewed and sucked the flesh down to the stone. He felt better, either because of the small amount of food or because of the miraculous reappearance of Emil, he wasn't sure which. Emil and two other Bosnian men stood a few yards away, looking down at the city. Trembling, unsteady, Gray got to his feet and walked over to them.

"What is going on?"

"The Serbs are deporting the people. Women and children into one set of buses, men into another." Emil handed Gray a set of binoculars. "What your media calls ethnic cleansing. The men are going to be executed."

"What has happened to the Bosnian Army?"

"Scattered," Emil said. "Most tried to break out. Everything is bad."

"What are you still doing here?" He handed the binoculars back to Emil.

Emil grinned at him, "We are volunteers."

Gray leaned against a tree, nodded. "Or did you all get lost?"

"One way to put it." He leaned close to Gray. "I also came looking for you."

"This is suicide."

"I do not plan on dying," Emil said.

"Neither do I, but look at me."

"Here." Emil took another plum out of a small satchel and handed it to Gray. "You'll feel better if you eat more."

They crept about on the hill throughout the day, watched people being loaded onto trucks. Emil and the others counted the shots fired from the areas where the men had been taken. They cursed the United Nations. The Serbs. The leaders of Europe and America.

Gray's own anger and impotence rose to the back of his throat like vomit. The image of the woman was always there when he closed his eyes. He couldn't tell them, couldn't put the event into words. Wasn't even sure anymore it would be wise to ever show the pictures. How could anyone believe he had been coerced into taking them and had not, somehow, granted permission for the act by his presence?

Finally something had crowded Lian out of his mind. His mind circled again and again around the woman, alone, trapped in her nightmare, ended by a single bullet.

"I should get a rifle," Gray said.

"You cannot fight."

"Is that an assessment of my shooting or a command?"

"Both."

"I'm a very good shot."

"Then it is a command. If the Serbs catch you armed, they will kill you no matter how many press cards you have."

"They may kill me anyway."

"True."

The Serbs stopped their deportations after the sun went down. Thousands of people were still left in and around the Dutch compound. Shots were still being fired in places.

Awake, recovering, Gray felt the others with Emil staring at him, assessing him like a strange insect. Their impotent rage, he knew, was turned toward him by virtue of his nationality. He'd heard it all before. *Why didn't the Americans press the Europeans to act?*

Gray kept himself separated from the small band and began conversations only with Emil. In the dark there was nothing to occupy him. He sat in the deeper shadows, a cigarette cupped in his hands to hide the glowing end. The cigarette cut the taste of plums in his mouth, and he thought about taking a shower, brushing his teeth, the over-starched sheets on hotel beds. He thought of the woman in the woods, alone.

He could have forgotten Lian if he hadn't come to this place, hadn't seen these things. The certainty of it pushed at his mind. A lack of danger shifts a person's values just as heavily as the omnipresence of death. He had hoped, once, that this war would erase Lian from his mind, that she would prove to be less important. He had hoped Suzzette would distract him. Those things, however, had proven to be only temporary, like the high from marijuana or the buzz from alcohol. The violence. The death. It was the sharpest of all contrasts. Each new atrocity that he saw made him long for the Lian he'd known before that night. The taste of her skin in his mouth.

"We are going down the hill," Emil whispered to him.

"Are you going to try and get out?"

"No, we want to get closer to that place northeast of the city. Toward Bratunac. It is important that you come."

"You want pictures."

"Yes."

"I can give you one of the cameras."

In the darkness Gray watched Emil turn, look over his shoulder at the other fighters. Then Emil turned back to him and leaned closer. "If you stay here, Gray, you will certainly die."

"You say that," Gray whispered, "but both of us might not have a choice in where and when we die."

"Do not be such a bloody cryptic cop."

"I'm being practical, Emil. There's no food, and we're on foot. That all narrows down our chances here."

"Are you saying you want to roll over like a dog?"

"No. Trying to keep our hopes from soaring out of control."

Emil nodded and placed a hand on Gray's shoulder. "I will buy the first round of drinks when we get back to Travnik."

"Well, as long as you're buying."

"You will have to get me that back pay first."

"Right. Of course."

They moved quietly in the dark, their packs and satchels tied down to their backs and sides to keep them from rattling around as they moved. A small moon slipped in and out of the clouds, revealing their stone faces in its pale light. They stopped and crouched close to the shadows on the ground, listened to the air and the sounds of gunfire. Someone was still fighting, the shots were too quick, too heavy to be the shots of executioners or suicides.

When clouds covered the moon they moved, drew closer to the place where they had heard the most shots the day before. They stopped, curled into the shadows of the trees around them, and waited while the two other men went ahead to check their path. They came back quickly.

"There are bodies everywhere, piled on top of each other," one of the men said.

Emil started to translate, and Gray stopped him. He had understood.

"We cannot take pictures in the dark," Emil said. "We would have to use a flash, and that would draw their attention."

"But they will be back in the morning," the man closest to Gray said.

"We will have to go quickly," Gray said in Bosnian, then in English he said, "Tell them I have two cameras, and you and I can take forty pictures in ten minutes as soon as the sun comes up."

Emil told them.

"And then we kill the Serbs who come back here." In the dark Gray could not tell who said that.

"You are small enough to slip away easily," Gray whispered.

"I am done running." The same voice, but having heard it a second time Gray was relieved that it was not Emil.

Gray tried to sleep against a tree near the killing fields, and when he couldn't sleep he stared out toward the field and thought about how he would arrive home.

He would return quietly, spend the first weeks in his apartment watching TV, and turn on the lights in the dead of night. He would bathe twice a day. Eat four meals. Then he would go and stand on the front porch of Lian's house, and he would . . . His mind always stopped there. Skipped in place like an old vinyl record. His idyll interrupted by the woman in the woods. Her withdrawn, distant look replacing everything he imagined. He tried to go back to the daydreams of luxury and rest, but she began to appear there as if she were the ghostly second image on double-exposed film.

The tension pulled him awake to a darkness slightly less black than sleep, and for a moment he wasn't sure he'd even opened his eyes until Emil whispered his name.

"It is not good to dream so deeply here."

"I'm sorry. I was dreaming of home," Gray whispered.

"I dream of home too."

"We can't die here, Emil. We can't let that happen."

"I understand."

"Let's take these pictures in the morning, then get out of here."

"It is a plan then?"

"As much of a plan as we have."

Gray rested quietly, watched the sky grow lighter as the sun came closer to the horizon. He knew they could speak of plans, pretend there was the certainty of their path. The truth was just as likely to be that they would walk unsuspecting into their graves the next day. The synchronicity of a man tripping a quarter mile away, his rifle going off, and the bullet traveling blindly, its trajectory planned for a spot Gray had not yet reached. The two moving to meet each other in the empty space of the future. The physics of chance.

***Sunrise is** my favorite time of day,* Lian said, her body pressed against his. The world around them turned blue-silver and then orange and red. *It lets me know I made it through another night.*

Are your nights so bad?

Not anymore.

He held her, watched the sunrise she loved over her shoulder. Something moving in the curtains. A flash of dark hair.

He watched this sunrise in Bosnia and thought of them both. Felt the night's unrest creep under the layer of sweat and grit on his skin and down to the center of his body. He reached up and felt the thick stubble on his chin and cheeks. The sensation made him aware of how old he felt. How crippled he had let himself become. When he could distinguish colors on the ground, he nudged Emil and handed him one of the backup cameras.

Gray left the camera bag under the tree and walked out of the woods and onto the killing field. The others crouched at the edge of the woods and watched. It was something out of a nightmare. Some of the bodies were already starting to bloat from the previous day's heat and had begun to turn black. The Serbs would have to get the bodies in the ground that day, or the smell would overtake everything for miles.

Slowly they circled the mass of bodies and took pictures carefully. Gray made sure there was a face in each photograph. Maybe it would help others close up their own mystery; let them grieve and move on.

"Gray." Emil's voice carried across the ocean of bodies, and Gray looked up. "Come here."

Gray took a picture, then walked quickly around to where Emil stood.

"It's the boy," Emil said.

"Fikret."

They stood over the boy's body, watched the wind move his hair. His eyes were open, filmed over and milky white. There were so many wounds. Someone had turned out the boy's pockets.

"I thought he was with the ones who got out," Gray said.

"I guess not."

Gray stood quietly, his hands holding a camera that suddenly felt heavy as a body.

"I need to get another roll of film," Emil said, and started back across the field.

Gray didn't stop him, but he was sure Emil had not burned through two rolls of film. Alone in the middle of a field of dead men, Gray felt something break loose inside him. He knelt down and took off his cap, placed it gently over the boy's face, and was about to whisper a prayer when he heard the truck engine.

No time. He stood and ran back to the trees; the sudden movement and fear pushed the weariness out of him. Revived with adrenaline, he leaped over a tree stump and slid on the ground to where Emil crouched near the camera bag. Emil pointed to the camera he held, made an okay sign with his hand, then picked up his rifle. Gray quickly stuffed everything into the bag, reloaded his camera, and changed to a telephoto lens before he zipped the bag shut and crawled up to where Emil was.

The truck appeared, followed by a bus loaded with Bosnian men. He could tell, even from a distance, that they were afraid, that they knew what was going to happen to them and that there was nothing they could do about it. Most prayed as they were taken off the bus. Some had soiled themselves. Others were paralyzed by fear or a sense of lingering resistance and had to be carried, kicked, and dragged to the edge of the kill zone. They were lined up and shot from behind, their bodies left to lie where they'd fallen.

The sound of another engine, deeper, and a Serbian soldier drove a large backhoe, spotted brown with rust, into the field. Gray took pictures, could hear the voices of the Bosnians hiding in the woods with him. Angry, barely whispers. They wanted to do something, were planning to ambush the execution squad. Their anger overcame their reason. He looked at Emil, knew he heard them as well. They would run as soon as the first shots were fired; they just didn't expect them to come so soon and so close.

He pushed himself to his feet, turned, and grabbed for the camera bag. The tree splintered above him, and he rolled away, swearing. The camera bag's strap tangled around his arm. He stood up, clutching the bag to his chest.

Emil was yards ahead of him, running blindly. He yelled Emil's name. Emil turned briefly and their eyes met, but it was as if he didn't see Gray at all. He was certain all Emil saw was the evil pursuing him. The threat of death. There was no way Gray could catch up to him, no way he could follow him through the woods. He clutched his bag and began to run. Then, suddenly, it seemed as if he were running through a swarm of wasps. The perception surreal until something took hold of his right shoulder and pushed him to the ground.

The pain appeared, a hot, horrible throb, and he wanted to lie there on the ground and cry. But he had to move, and he pushed himself up, held his right arm with his left, and ran deeper into the woods. He needed to find someplace to hide, someplace to disappear.

He saw blackness. A tree had fallen across another tree, and bushes had grown up, making a small bower. It would do, if he hurried. The wasps were coming back. He had to hurry. He collapsed under the fallen trees, slipped out of consciousness.

Later, awake in darkness, he could not remember when the fighting had stopped. He woke because of the dull pain in his shoulder. He tried to listen for the sound of people. The suggestions of pursuit.

When he was sure no one was around, he began to worry about his arm. Gray didn't think the wound itself was that bad, but if he didn't get it taken care of, he would die of gangrene. He was sure he could make it to Potočari, but he would have to find his way through the Serbs to get to the UN battalion that was certainly still there, and he wasn't sure if he still had his credentials with him. The camera bag was gone, dropped somewhere after he had been shot. There was no way he could find it in the dark.

Moving made the pain worse, and when he sat up he felt dizzy. He sat very still, his eyes focused on the moon rising, its pale body cut into slices by the brush that grew over him. *Five minutes,* he thought, *five minutes and I'll get up and leave.*

Then he heard something moving through the grass. Gray wanted to call out, beg for help, but the sound could belong to anything. Animals. Survivors. Serbs. Why hadn't they chased him down? Had they not seen him, or Emil? After a moment the sound went away. It had probably been an animal, or the wind.

He was sure ghosts would be spoken of in this place. The owners of the bones piled in mass graves, or lost in the dense grass and trees, would always hover here. He did not want to be one of them. Exhausted, he lay down, telling himself he needed just a few more moments to gather his strength, and fell asleep.

It was hours before he awoke again, brought out of sleep by the pain in his shoulder, and something else. A presence next to him. Without opening his eyes, he could tell it was day. The sunlight was warm against his face. The brightness illuminated the blood vessels in his eyelids. Slowly he opened his eyes and let them adjust to the brightness until he could see the old woman who knelt over him. A bloody rag in one hand. A long, thin knife in the other. She made a noise like soothing a baby and put the knife aside.

"I took out the bullet," she said in Bosnian.

"Thank you."

"I heard you talking. I did not think anyone would be alive here."

"Are you alone?"

"Not anymore."

"It is dangerous."

"Everyone is gone, and only the most evil would kill a *kaluderica*."

"I do not know that word," he said.

She held her hands together as if praying.

"A nun," he said in English. *"Kaluderica."*

"Yes. Can you walk? It is not a short journey to my home, but it is not long either."

"I can try. I need to find my cameras."

"There will be time later. After you have healed."

Coming Home

Jack sits alone in his room at the Holiday Inn and stares out the window at the dark mountains around Sarajevo. Lian and Daniel are down the hall from him, but he already feels cut away, alone. During the trip back to Sarajevo, he dwelled on the idea that, if he'd been there with them, Gray might still be alive. Or they could both be dead.

He knows it is only wishful thinking. *Gray must be dead,* he tells himself. A cluster of bones lost among thousands of clusters of bones. What was he doing at his age believing himself to be invincible?

Jack gets up, leans on his cane, and feels for his flask. It's empty. He drops it on the bed and turns to leave the room. For a moment he considers calling Lian, asking her down for a drink. A belated wake for Gray. He decides against it. She has too many of her own problems. He opens the door and steps into the hallway.

A light flickers on the ceiling a few doors down, losing the end of the hallway to occasional darkness and shadows. In a spasm of light

Jack thinks he sees someone, but then in the next flash there is nothing. He turns and limps down the hall to the elevator.

During his ride down to the lobby, he thinks Veronica was right. It is time to retire, collect his pension, and try to get to know his daughter despite her apparent dislike of him. He could try to talk to Veronica again, even though she seems determined to avoid him. He could stop drinking. *Just not tonight,* he thinks as the elevator doors open.

He steps out of the elevator and goes across the lobby to the lounge, where he sees Emil sitting alone at a table, a drink in front of him.

"I suppose you don't mind me joining you?"

"Please, Jack, sit down."

"I was coming down to have a few drinks myself."

"I was wondering how long it would take you."

"Let's order another round and have a proper wake," Jack says and waves to a waitress. She comes over, takes their orders, and leaves.

"Katja is not sure she wants to leave Sarajevo," Emil says. "She thinks I am not yet over Mira."

"And my wife divorced me," Jack says.

"We should start a club."

"Already have, Emil. Already have."

The waitress brings their drinks and sets them on the table. Jack holds his glass up, looks at the ice swirling in the pale scotch. "Let's hope we do things right from here on out."

"Or at least better than in the past," Emil says.

They drink and plunk the glasses down on the table, sit looking at each other. Jack clears his throat, puts his elbows on the table, and leans forward.

"What happened out there, Emil?"

"Gray ran out of luck," he says. "I ran out of courage. That is all I can say, Jack."

Jack nods. "I wish we had found something."

"Here," Emil says and takes the roll of film out of his shirt pocket, then picks up the camera off the floor. "It was in with Stjepan's things. What would a blind boy need with a camera and a roll of film?"

"You think they're Gray's?"

"I try not to think anything anymore," Emil says. "Take it with you. Develop it, and send me copies of the prints."

Jack holds the canister close to his ear and shakes it. "Could be there's nothing on it."

"True."

"I should have brought my kit," Jack says. "You don't suppose they still have the darkroom?"

"No."

"A mystery," he says and shakes the canister again, not wanting to admit he is excited at the prospect.

Lian is curled up on the foot of Daniel's bed while he sits in a chair by the table. Their conversation has been choppy and sporadic. Broad statements have been made that Lian is sure have something to do with accusation and doubt. There is silence as she tries to determine how much he hurts and how much he has begun to hate her. For the first time since she has known him, he slouches.

"You still haven't said whether you want a divorce," she says.

"I don't know, Lian."

She closes her eyes. The sound of their breathing irritates her. The tone of Daniel's voice when he says anything, as if it were a knife he tries to jab her with, makes her wish she had stayed in her own room and gone to bed.

He takes off his glasses and rubs the bridge of his nose. His aggravated gesture. It means he won't give her a definite answer. Not now. She reminds herself to be patient with him, but as she lies there watching Daniel massage away his urge to be emotional, she is unable to open her mouth and say what he needs to hear from her.

"I should go now," she says instead.

Slowly she stands up from the bed and goes to the door. The carpet is rough and scratches the bottoms of her bare feet. When she reaches for the doorknob, Daniel clears his throat.

"I'll try to give you an answer before we leave."

"Whenever you're ready, Daniel."

She opens the door and steps into the hallway. As she walks to her room she looks over her shoulder toward the far end of the hallway, where the light flickers on and off. The area of darkness beyond the flickering light feels haunted. She stops at her door and feels the pockets of her jeans for the key. She finds it and lets herself into the room.

It would be impossible to sleep, she realizes as she stands looking at the bed. There is little else to do in the room. *With any luck,* she thinks, *Jack will be downstairs in the lounge and we can have a drink or two.* After she puts her shoes on, she leaves her room and walks quickly to the elevators, away from the darkness at the other end of the hall.

In the lounge she is a little surprised to see Emil. He and Jack are already on their way to being drunk.

"We're having a wake," Jack says.

"Good," she says and drags a chair over to their table, sits down.

They nod, look down at their drinks, then both turn their heads to look for the waitress.

It took some time, but Katja has finally found the plot in the cemetery where Stjepan was buried while she was gone, chasing after Emil. She sits down next to the small marker and closes her eyes.

She won't talk to the headstone, hates the ridiculousness of trying to throw sound at the dead. However, she does wish somehow to apologize for not having been there, for letting him be buried by strangers. She wants to apologize for being the one who came after Mira in Emil's heart and knows how strange such an apology would sound, as if it were an apology for wanting to be loved.

When she opens her eyes she sees a man standing a few yards away, the upper half of his body hidden in the shadow of the tunnel that leads under the old bleachers to the soccer pitch. His presence unsettles her, and she looks around for a way out. When she looks at the man in the tunnel again, he raises his right hand into the moonlight, fingers out, then turns and walks into the darker shadows. There seems something familiar about the gesture, and she wishes it were daylight so she could have seen his face. Maybe it was someone she knew.

She stays by Stjepan's grave a little longer, thinking her silent apologies to the boy, and then gets up to go. The nearest exit is the tunnel where the man was in the shadows. She approaches the tunnel cautiously. Peering into the shadows for his image, she takes a few steps into the tunnel where he stood and kicks something on the ground.

She crouches in the shadows and finds it, drags it out into the moonlight. It is a weathered camera bag with a broken zipper. Inside is a broken camera, its body apparently shattered by a bullet. Frantically, half dreading, half wishing, she searches the pockets and compartments of the bag, looking for anything else. The bag is empty; it could have belonged to anyone, at any time.

She almost calls out Gray's name, but she feels ridiculous and haunted. She puts the bag back on the ground where she found it, then kicks it away and walks quickly out of the cemetery.

In her mind she tries to make a list of things she will need to take with her if she is to live with Emil. He is right; there are too many ghosts in Sarajevo.

They walk with Jack to his room. Lian tries to avoid looking into the darkness at the far end of the hallway, where the light has finally stopped working. She keeps her hand on Jack's arm as he searches his pockets for his key.

"Are you sure you do not want to come with us?" Emil asks.

"Yes, certainly. I am tired of walking."

He finds his key and shows it to them before unlocking the door. Emil helps Jack into the room, and Lian waits. Staring down at the darkness at the end of the hallway, she expects someone to be there, for that person to step slowly into the light. Finally she looks away, afraid of who it might be, and enters Jack's room.

Jack has already sprawled across the bed, but he isn't asleep. Lian watches his eyes track something across the ceiling. When she looks up, there is nothing there.

"It's been a delight," Jack says. "Too bad we didn't find anything more."

"Perhaps I hoped for too much," Emil says.

"I've always hated it when people told me never to hope too much, as if it were some finite currency and shouldn't be wasted. I hate to be obvious here, but if you're miserly with hope, aren't you then, eventually, hopeless?"

He raises his face and winks at Lian. "The wisdom of a drunk," he says and pulls a pillow underneath his head.

"Do you need anything before we go?" Lian asks.

"No. No, I don't believe so."

"I will see you tomorrow then," Emil says.

"Yes."

Lian turns, leads Emil out of the room, and waits as he pulls the door shut. Together they walk down the hall, away from the darkness at the other end. Once, before they step into the elevator, Lian looks back, tries to see through the darkness there. A movement maybe, or a trick of the eyes. A hand raised in the blackness, then the illusion is gone.

Outside, the sky turns gray as dawn begins to push itself over the horizon. Lian walks with Emil and looks at the buildings along the street. In this light the war damage does not seem as bad, the raw wounds hidden by the shadows. It is easy to imagine the old, uninjured Sarajevo. The city reminds her of pictures she has seen of wounded soldiers, their shoulders thrown back, chins up, almost oblivious to the empty pant leg or shirt sleeve.

Since leaving the hotel Emil has not spoken, and she has not tried to make him. There is only the sound of their shoes on the pavement. The occasional car. Other footsteps that seem to vanish when Lian turns to look. Soon the buildings they walk past are older, their damage more severe. Whole walls have been stripped away, revealing the rooms that once housed families, lovers, the lonely. Everything is now in the transition from rubble back to buildings.

"There," Emil says, points toward the tall, thin minaret and the two green-capped domes of the mosque. "Gazi Husref Bey."

"It's beautiful," she says.

Emil leads her closer to the mosque while the sun begins to unfold itself from behind the mountains. From somewhere else in the city, an amplified voice rises from one mosque, then another, moving through the city as if to land there in front of them as a voice rises from the Gazi Husref Bey.

"They are calling the faithful to pray," Emil says.

"They sound sad."

"Yes."

They enter the mosque through a narrow gate. Scaffolds climb up walls in midrepair, among piles of stone and heavy construction tools. Emil leads her to the mosque's fountain, where she watches him remove two collapsible cups from the pockets of his old army jacket, then reach through the iron bars. He dips both into the water and hands one to her.

"There is a legend," Emil says. "The legend says that if you drink from the well at the Gazi Husref Bey, you will always return to Sarajevo."

"Did you bring Gray here?"

"Yes. And now you. Perhaps," he says, "the legend might work for me just once."

Lian holds the small cup of water, unable to share her doubts with him, unable to stop the lightning slash of hope. When Emil raises his cup to her, she smiles and brings the cup to her lips.

"What will you do when you return home?" Emil asks.

She shrugs, holding the cup with both hands, and looks into the clear water.

"I don't suppose there is much to do," she says. "I mean, he's gone one way or another, isn't he?"

"There are days when I would give anything to have Mira back. I know in my mind that it can never be, but the heart is slow to surrender."

"I cannot stay with Daniel. It's not the same."

"Then do not stay with him. Maybe your story will be different."

She swallows the last bit of water in her cup and gives it back to Emil. "My story is different," she says. "Nothing came between us except me."

He feels predatory. Jealous. Criminal.

Unable to sleep, he left his room and wandered the hotel most of the night. It was chance that put him in a position to watch them leave the hotel without being seen. Perhaps if he hadn't still been so restless, or if he hadn't thought himself in circles most of the night, he wouldn't have followed them. Now, standing in the shrinking shadows of a gutted building, he watches his wife and Emil as they appear again at the narrow gate and stand talking.

A few people walk past the spot where he is trying to squeeze himself into the last bit of darkness. They are drawn forward by the voice calling out from the mosque, most with their heads down. A few see him in the shadows, nod in his direction.

Church bells begin to ring.

"Amazing, isn't it?" someone says.

Daniel turns to find the person who spoke to him. The man stands on the sidewalk and leans against the wall where it meets the doorway Daniel is hiding in.

"What is amazing?"

"This city. These people. Hemingway once said something about the Spanish being the best and the worst people. I think the Bosnians are also the best and the worst. I've seen them kill their neighbors like they were butchering a cow, and I've seen them risk their lives to save someone they don't know."

"It seems pretty universal, actually," Daniel says.

"Yes, I'm sure it is. But the observer tends to love the ones he has observed the most, don't you think?"

Daniel shrugs, glances back toward the mosque. Emil and Lian are still standing just outside the gate. He wonders if he should leave now, go back to the hotel before they do, or if he should stay and talk to this man.

"There is a legend about that mosque," the man says.

"Can it resurrect the dead?"

"No. The legend is that if you drink from the well inside, you will always return to Sarajevo. That is why I am here. Why are you here?"

"That is my wife."

"Are you waiting for her, or spying on her?"

"That's not really any of your business."

"You're right. I apologize. It's just been so long since I've spoken to another American," the man says.

Daniel watches the man reach into a coat pocket, take out a pack of cigarettes, then a folded, wrinkled envelope.

"Would you do another American a favor?" he says and holds the envelope out to Daniel. "Give this to the man she is with."

"Why don't you?"

The man shrugs. "It's a long story that ended somewhere else," he says, then smiles. "And I don't think he's quite ready to see me, even if he thinks he is. What's in there will help him, though. Please, I've got to go."

Daniel accepts the envelope as the man pushes himself away from the wall and walks off. He moves easily through the other people as if they were trees. Daniel steps out of the doorway, thinking for a moment that he will follow the man and give it back to him, but he doesn't. He stands in the street, an island the people drifting to worship flow around.

"Daniel?"

He stops and turns to see his wife and Emil coming down the street toward him.

"I'm sorry, I was following you."

"Are you going to follow me forever?"

He finds that he can't answer her. She shakes her head and pushes past him, walks down the street by herself. Daniel watches her for a moment, then looks back at Emil where he still stands with his hands in his pockets.

"I think he was here. He gave me this and said I should give it to you." Daniel holds out the envelope to Emil.

"Where did he go?"

"Down that alley," Daniel says.

Emil takes the envelope. "Thank you."

"Aren't you going to follow him?"

"No, not today," Emil says, opening the envelope.

Daniel's concern rises as Emil unfolds the paper inside, then suddenly buckles and sits down with his back against the building.

"What's wrong?" he asks.

"It's a list of identified remains," he says. "My fiancée's name is on it."

Daniel sits down next to him and waits quietly.

Gray follows Lian from the next street over, knows the route she will take back to the Holiday Inn and is not worried at the long stretches between alleys when he cannot see her. He hurries to the intersection where she will have to turn to get back to the hotel, leans against a wall there that still bears the painted warning PAZI SNAJPER, and waits for her to appear.

When she turns the corner, he is paralyzed for a moment. She walks with her head down, her arms folded across the top of her stomach. It has been so long, and doubt has crept closer to him. He never expected to see her here, even after he'd learned Emil was looking for him.

When Suzzette had written to him that the War Crimes Tribunal would accept Gray's photographs and the names of the men who had raped the woman in the woods, she had also mentioned receiving a letter from Emil. He had asked her not to write to Emil. There were still things he needed to do. Promises to keep. And he did not yet want to deal with Emil, the unresolved things between them.

The woman in the photograph has come to help him. We all thought you were dead.

It does not matter, he had told Stjepan then, his mind locked down on the miserable promise he wished he'd never made.

But it has mattered, he thinks. The knowledge that Lian has come here, despite believing him dead, has changed the course and purpose of his trajectory out of Bosnia. Lian, coming here by chance to meet him, has sped up everything, and the swing of emotions, from despair to joy, has filled those places he'd emptied in that bower before the old Franciscan sister saved him and protected him from the Serbs.

Finally he pushes away from the wall and starts walking toward Lian. As he approaches, he watches her, waits for her to recognize him, but she won't look up. He wants to say something as they pass, anything to make her look up at him, but each idea is rejected until she unfolds her arms and lets them swing at her sides. As they pass he reaches out to let his left hand brush against the back of her left hand.

He stops after a few more steps, turns, and watches her as she stops and stands still. Quietly he waits for her to turn around and look at him. When she does, he sees she is crying. They stand silently for a few moments, the space between them refusing to close.

"Why didn't you come home?"

"What would I have come home to?" he asks.

She wipes the damp streaks off her face, folds her arms again as if she is trying to keep things from falling out of her stomach.

"I don't know," she says. "I couldn't bring myself to leave him until I thought you were dead."

"After I was shot," he says, and sees her flinch, "I lay out there in the woods listening to other people die. When those sounds went away, I was sure I would die too. So I began to talk to the trees and the shadows. That's how Tana found me, mumbling about things to the darkness."

He lets a silence fill the space between them, giving her room to speak if she wants, but Lian stands there, still holding herself. Silent.

"She carried me out of there; she saved me. Allowed me a second chance," he says.

"Do you love her?"

"Yes."

She nods, starts to turn away.

"It's not that kind of love, Lian," he says, and she stops again.

"Don't torture me," she says. "Please."

With her back to him, his eyes focus on her shoulder and the place where he bit her. The memory strikes him, a hammer blow to his insides. "Everything's done except this one thing," he says.

Lian turns around to look at him again.

It seems as if they are trapped in place, unable to move any closer. Just these sharp pirouettes in place. He sees her clutching the fabric of her shirt against her ribs, her crossed arms writhing like snakes. She is wrestling with something, and he lets her, willing to take whatever she offers. Finally he moves a step closer, bringing the subtle changes to her face into clearer focus. She seems thinner, and there are tiny creases around her eyes that were not there before. Her face is that of someone who has been unhappy for too long. There is an echo of remorse. A swell of tenderness.

"What am I supposed to do now?" she asks.

"I can't answer that question for you, Lian."

She unfolds her arms, lets them drop to her waist where she holds her right index finger tightly in her left fist. She looks away, into the sunrise. Gray watches her, tries to discern the shape and texture of her thoughts by the way her mouth is set, the movement of her eyes. But she is still now.

Sunlight touches them as they stand rooted to this piece of distance between them. They make an island of stillness among the growing stream of people emerging from the buildings around them. People's voices, the clatter on the pavement, the sound of cars make Gray lean closer to her, afraid that when she speaks it will be too softly for him to hear.

When she looks at him again she is suddenly unfamiliar.

"Can we go home now?" she asks.

He takes a deep breath; it seems the deepest in years. "I don't know where that is anymore," he says.

"Anywhere we want," she answers him.

Acknowledgments

Although this work refers to actual people, events, and locations, it is ultimately a work of my imagination and therefore unreliable as a source of historical record. For the facts, there were a number of authors whose books were indispensable to me and deserve to be noted. Ed Vulliamy's *Seasons in Hell: Understanding Bosnia's War,* Dzevad Karahasan's *Sarajevo: Exodus of a City,* Naza Tanovic-Miller's *Testimony of a Bosnian,* Chuck Sudetic's *Blood and Vengeance: One Family's Story of The War in Bosnia,* Jan Willem Honig's *Srebrenica: Record of a War Crime,* and Anthony Loyd's *My War Gone By, I Miss It So.* Also important were Eric Liu's *The Accidental Asian: Notes of a Native Speaker* and Claire S. Chow's *Leaving Deep Water: Asian American Women at the Crossroads of Two Cultures.*

There are a number of people for whom I am very grateful. Connie Jobe and Rebecca Maglaughlin were important teachers early in life who encouraged me to write. Steve Heller and Jonathan Holden at Kansas State University, Reed Bye, Anne Waldman, Keith Abbott, Junior

Burke, Kristen Iversen, and especially Bobbie Louise Hawkins at Naropa University who all challenged and enlightened me in one way or another. My humble thanks to Gary Clift for the constant encouragement and letters of recommendation and to Alexs D. Pate for cramming so much important knowledge into one week of class and a long dinner over sushi and sake in the summer of 2000.

Thank you to Caitlin, Rachel, Laural, and everyone at Unbridled Books. As for Fred Ramey, he has my undying loyalty and affection for believing in this book and its untested, unknown author.

And finally, for their time and intelligence, for providing me with dinners and beers and letting me rant and storm about the world of writing and my place in it, I offer my deepest gratitude to the following people: Mac and Brenda Welch, Deena Wade, Kimberly Thompson-Gerlach, Jaime Lott, Karyn Hardy and Todd Seiffert, Jenn Zukowski-Boughn, Evan Hundhousen, Gavin Pate, and Rebekah Rine. Delia Tramontina served as an early reader and, at times, an unpaid therapist during the early stages of this book. If not for the constant friendship and intellectual challenge provided by Laura Hawley, I'm not sure this book would have taken the shape it did.

A final thank you goes to my parents, Eunice and Dennis, and my sister, Amber, for helping to support me over the last nineteen years with emergency money, shelter, and food. Without them I would be homeless and malnourished several times over.